Christma.
Leaves of Change
Café

By Sarah L
Campbell

Sarah L Campbell

Book One in The
Leaves of Change
Café Series

Copyright ©2021 Sarah Louise Campbell

This is a work of fiction. Names, characters, places, and incidents are either products of the author's imagination or used fictitiously. Any resemblance to actual persons, living or dead, or real places or events is coincidental and unintended by the author.

ISBN (paperback) 978-1-8383474-0-6

Dear Reader,

Thank you for choosing my book. Can you believe that Christmas is once upon us again? It hardly seems like five minutes ago since last Christmas when the eBook first came out. The reviews that came from that first book gave me the confidence to keep writing about Aurora and her family and friends.

I hope that you'll enjoy this first book in the series, a cosy read full of festive fun. Merry Christmas to you

Love

Sarah x

Dedication page

For Mum,

Thank you for all the love and support you have given me during this writing process. Without you, none of my books would have come to fruition. xx

To Louie,

You may just be a cat but without you, my life would not be complete. Thank you for making my day a little bit brighter with your cuddles and companionship. xx

To the reader,

Thank you so much for buying my book. Every book sold means the world to me. I am honoured that you chose to read my book.

Sarah xx

Chapter One

I locked the door of my home for the last time. A detached Victorian house that wouldn't look out of place on a picture postcard. Its beautiful bay windows stretched out onto the lawn. The garden with its glorious apple tree. I'd spent many sunny days sitting underneath it.

"Goodbye," I said, closing the gate and touching the white fence I'd lovingly painted. I choked back tears. Silly really, but I couldn't help get sentimental. Fifteen years I had lived there with my husband, Nick. I turned to the new owners with their beaming smiles. Now it would be their laughter ringing through the walls; their coats hung up in the cupboard. Somehow, I put my thoughts to one side and greeted them with as much of a smile as I could muster.

"Good luck with the baby, Aurora," they said in unison.

"Thanks," I said, putting a hand on my protruding stomach. "Enjoy the house." I handed over the keys and turned towards the car with tears in my eyes.

I climbed in the car and watched them eagerly going inside. All I could think about was the day that we were married and Nick insisted on carrying me over the threshold. It was cliché I know, but I loved it, both of us laughing and thinking we had our entire lives ahead.

I drove away and the picture blurred in my mind as the rain pelted against my windscreen. I realised the memory was of another Nick, another me. Another life. A kick inside my stomach brought me out of myself. I couldn't lose myself in memories or else I would drown. I had to fight, somehow rise from the ashes of all that I once was and begin again.

"We don't need him, do we?" I said to the baby inside me. I turned up the radio and thought about Green Leaf, the town I had left at nineteen. The kind of small-town where everybody knows everybody's business.

I swore that I would never go back there. But I

had no choice. Since Nick had left, I couldn't afford the mortgage on our dream house anymore. Not on my unstable salary as an actress, and as my stomach grew, there were only a certain number of roles for a pregnant lady.

I had friends in London, mainly Nick's. They weren't the kind I could rely on at a time like this. Mum was my only family, so, like it or lump it, I had to sell the house and go back home.

Three hours and two stops at a service station later, I saw the sign: *Welcome to Green Leaf, the town where the leaves are always changing.*

I drove along the little seafront, turning up to the high street where Christmas was in full swing. The street lamps with their curls of green tinsel wrapped tightly around and the shops with their festive lights in the windows. I passed by the artsy and gift shops. Then finally the bookshop: Green Sleeves. I pulled the car up next door to it at The Leaves of Change Café. Mum had run it by herself since my grandma passed.

I turned off the engine and glanced back at the bookshop. My stomach tightened as Michael Morday, my old teenage boyfriend, came to the door to change the sign from open to closed. Apart from a streak of grey in the middle of his brown crown of hair, he hadn't changed at all.

Those green eyes, which in the right light looked almost emerald. He wore a smart blue shirt and dark blue jeans.

I knew he owned the bookshop, but I hadn't expected to see him so soon. It was easy to see the boy he once was. The boy I had fallen in love with.

Come on Aurora, I told myself, *no point in dwelling on the past.* I took a few deep breaths and turned back towards the café. I put on my lipstick like I was applying war paint. *Right, you can do this, Aurora. It's only your mother.* Desperate for the bathroom, I couldn't wait any longer. I got out of the car, my legs as heavy as my mood.

A familiar jangle of the café bell announced my arrival. Customers turned to greet me. Lots of faces I recognised; everyone from my old school teacher to the town mayor, grey-haired now. A few others I couldn't quite place. Tourists probably. Doubtless Mum knew all of their business, even if they had just come to town. She was a fast worker.

I gawped at the Christmas tree in the corner, decorated with enough tacky ornaments and lights to rival a shopping centre. A thick snake of tinsel around the cabinets and the chintzy plates hanging on the wall. The lemon wallpaper and the small round tables with their plastic flowers were almost the same. Only, instead of pink tulips, their pots were filled with poinsettias.

A familiar gingerbread and cinnamon smell wafted my way from the counter. Mum stood behind it with her frilly apron on and a batch of freshly iced gingerbread biscuits in her hand. In front of her, was the display cabinet filled to the brim with Christmas and gingerbread biscuits, cinnamon rolls, muffins, fudge brownies and mince pies. They sat proudly on plates next to turntables of rich dark chocolate and white chocolate cheesecakes.

"There you are," said Mum, looking me up and down.

"Yes, here, I am," I replied, already feeling tense.

I went around the other side of the counter and gave her an awkward hug.

"You could have rung or sent me a message," she said, with a worried frown.

"Yes, sorry Mum," I said, breaking away from her. "My phone went flat." Under her gaze, I felt like a teenager again, caught out for telling lies about going to a party.

"I see," she murmured and raised her eyebrows. "You should do something with your hair other than tying it up in a frizzy brown mess."

"You went all out with the decorations again," I said, glancing back at the Christmas tree, ignoring her last remark.

"Well," she said. "The customers like it. I try to bring a little festive cheer to the café."

"I can see. I've had a long trip, I'm going upstairs to freshen up," I said, turning towards the side door that led up the stairs to the flat.

"Well, be quick about it and I'll have something ready for you to eat when you come back downstairs. Goodness only knows what rubbish you've been eating at the service station."

"I'm not hungry," I protested.

Mum sighed in disapproval. "Aurora, you've got to think of the baby."

"Fine," I said, rolling my eyes. I'd only been

back for five minutes and already she was bossing me about. Something else that hadn't changed.

On my return, I sat down as far away from the counter as possible and tried to ignore the customers' eyes on me. Doubtless with Nick being in the public eye, they knew everything that had happened between us.

A woman on the next table caught my eye. "When are you due?" she asked.

"Christmas Eve," I said, glancing at her and the small children beside her. A baby who couldn't have been more than six months old in the double pushchair and a toddler in a highchair next to her. It dawned on me who she was. "Rachel Pewter?" I asked, surprised to see my teenage best friend and closest ally against the world still in Green Leaf. She had told me enough times, she wanted to get away from this town as much as me.

"It's Rachel Bee now," she said. "Married Darren. He's the local chef at The Greyhound in Evergreen."

No wonder I couldn't find her online. "I can't believe that you married him," I said, thinking of the spindly, spotty boy, who mumbled every time that he tried to talk to us.

"I can't believe it either, but you should see him now. He's really blossomed." That I found hard to believe.

"You look the same," she noted.

"Oh, give over," I laughed. "Apart from the wrinkles and my massive stomach."

"No, you look great, glowing in fact."

"Sweating more like."

Both of us laughed.

"Here," said Mum, bringing me over a slab of lasagne with a side of vegetables. It was big enough to feed four.

I pulled a face, not sure that I could manage a quarter of it.

Mum shook her head at me. "Well, don't look like I've smacked you in the face, it'll be good for you."

She sat down at the table beside me, closely watching me eat. Rachel's smallest child cried her double pushchair.

Mum picked up her little elephant rattle that had fallen on the floor and gave it back to her. She smiled at Rachel and glanced back to the baby. "This little one is looking a lot better. Got over your runny nose, haven't you?" Mum said in a babyish voice.

Two customers came in. "Trust Patricia to be off on one of our busiest days," Mum muttered as she got up to serve them.

I remembered Patricia; a young mother, always coming to work with one of her kids in tow. They must be adults by now and Patricia would be nearing retirement age.

I turned back to Rachel and smiled. "I can't believe you have babies." When I looked at her, it was like it was yesterday and we were teenagers again.

"Yes, me either. This little monkey beside me is Maisie and her sister Rosie is in the double pushchair."

"Aww," I said, looking at them both. "They're adorable and I see Maisie inherited her mother's strawberry blonde curls."

"Yes, Rosie's got her father's light blonde hair." She paused and smiled sadly at me. "I didn't think I'd see you back here, Aurora?"

"No, I didn't expect that I would come back here," I shrugged. "But needs must."

"Yes," she said, her eyes full of sympathy. "I read in *Stars* magazine about you and Nick Hope. I'm sorry."

"Thanks," I said, swallowing a lump in my throat. She wouldn't be the last person to mention Nick. I'd have to get better at handling it. I looked down at my stomach as the baby kicked inside me.

"Ah," she said, following my gaze. "The little one is giving you no peace then I take it? Mine were the same and they've never stopped." As if on cue, Maisie pulled at Rachel's jumper sleeve and cried, "Mummy, Mummy, go home."

"Yes, I can see," I smiled.

"Yes Maisie," Rachel said. "We'll go home now."

Maisie grinned. "Yes, home now."

"Well," Rachel said, putting her in the double pushchair in front of her sister. "I'd better get her home, she's cranky if she doesn't get her afternoon nap. I'm up at Cloverfield Cottage. Why don't you come and visit us sometime?"

"Will do," I said. We swapped numbers before she left. I smiled, thinking that seeing her again was at least one good thing about being back in Green Leaf.

Chapter Two

Mum had kept everything the same in my old bedroom. The walls were still painted in their shocking pink, adorned with posters of boy bands I had worshipped. I could still name every member of each one and vividly remembered dancing around the room to their songs.

I turned to my dressing table and smiled at the photos forming a border around it. Some were of Rachel and me with paper hats on at Christmas; one was of us in our prom dresses. I spotted one of Michael and me at the beach, smiling from ear to ear, his arms around my waist. I climbed under the covers in my old bed, moving my teddy bears out of the way.

My thoughts started to drift... if I hadn't left for Uni, would Michael and I have had a chance to make things right? Tears came to my eyes and I shrugged them away. Beneath me, the hubbub of the café was still in full swing. I thought of Mum's expression when I arrived. She hadn't looked thrilled to see me. Had it all been a mistake to come back here?

The sound of heavy footsteps up the stairs echoed through my walls. Probably just Mum, I assumed. Then, I heard mumbling, a deep masculine voice, definitely not Mum. But who? A burglar? I reached for my phone and cursed, realising it was out of battery.

Out of the corner of my eye, I caught sight of an old hairbrush on the dressing table. Not exactly the best way to defend yourself against a burglar, but having nothing better to hand it would have to do. I sighed and tiptoed towards the bedroom door clutching it tightly in my hand and peered through the gap in my door. Across the landing, the living room door was only slightly ajar. I could see nothing but the shadow of the TV.

I snuck across the landing and stood with my back to the living room door. "I'm armed," I cried. "Show yourself." My tone was a tad overdramatic, I guess my acting skills came in handy then.

"Aurora, is that you?" came a gruff voice from

inside.

I opened the door and saw a strange grey-headed man dressed in a polo shirt and jeans, lounging on the sofa. I noted his shoe-less feet up on the coffee table like he owned the place. He took them down and sat bolt upright. "Sorry," he said, with a smile creeping up on his lips. "Don't throw the hairbrush at me, I'm Colin, your mum's er...friend."

"Right," I said, looking from him to the large moccasins that sat snuggly under the table and the array of men's clothes behind him on the radiator. Obviously more than a friend.

"I'm Aurora," I said, lowering my hairbrush.

He stood up and shook my hand. "Yes, your

mum told me you were coming. I didn't mean to give you a fright. Do you want to sit down?"

"No thanks," I said, fuming that Mum hadn't bothered to tell me about him. I marched back downstairs to have a word with Mum and found her cleaning the counter.

She glanced at me and then went back to her task. "I thought you were going for a lie-down?"

"Mum, can I have a word with you?"

Mum held the cloth in one hand and placed her hand on her hip with the other. "Yes?"

"When were you going to tell me about Colin?"

A look of relief spread across her face. "So that's what this is about. Honestly, darling, you make a lot of fuss over nothing. If you'd given me half a chance to explain then I would have told you about him." She looked like she was going to burst out laughing. "Anyway, it's hardly front-page news, is it? Hmm? Catherine Winter, proprietor of *The Leaves of Change Café* gets a boyfriend."

"Glad you're finding this so hilarious," I said. "I doubt that you would have found it so funny if you'd been me and found a strange man in the middle of your mum's living room."

"If you must know, I often did, your grandfather. I always thought that he was a little strange."

"Mum," I glared at her. "You really should have

told me about Colin."

"Look," she said, continuing to wash the counter. "You're a fine one to talk - I didn't even know you were pregnant until I read about it in that celebrity magazine, *Stars* or whatever it is. Anyway, Colin and I have been together for two years. If you'd called me more or at least bothered to visit me once in a while then you would know about it."

"I was busy living my own life," I snapped back. If I was honest with myself, it was more than that. I was just sick of her trying to take over every detail of my life. Mine and Nick's wedding for instance. She told me I should have held the wedding in Green Leaf and not in London, the bridesmaids should wear peach and not the gorgeous strapless lilac dresses I had chosen. Mum got her way about that, but when she tried to tell me how to run my own house, I stuck up for myself. That caused a lot of arguments, so eventually, I decided to stop calling her. It was easier that way.

Both of us turned to see Colin standing in the doorway, looking sheepish.

"Look," he said, "if you want some time for yourselves, then I can go home. I wouldn't want to get in the way of anything."

"Certainly not," Mum said, looking straight at me like *I* was the one being unreasonable. "Aurora may be my daughter but she doesn't live here. She'll just have to take as she finds."

"Right," he said, hastily retreating back through the side door.

"Look, I'm exhausted," I said. "I don't want to argue with you anymore, Mum."

"Fine," she said and picked up a tea towel. She threw it on her shoulder and took some plates to the kitchen.

"Fine," I grumbled. I went up to the flat and cursed myself for thinking we might get on for five minutes.

Chapter Three

I didn't know how much I would miss having my own space until I spent the evening playing gooseberry with Colin and Mum. The two of them cosying up on the sofa, arms around each other and watching banal TV programmes. I made my excuses to go to bed and had just started drifting off when I heard them giggling like newlyweds through the wall. Safe to say I didn't get much sleep.

Bleary-eyed, the following morning, I stumbled into the bathroom to find Colin naked in front of the mirror, shaving.

"Argh," I cried, shielding my eyes and backing

out the door. I don't know who was redder in the face, me or Colin.

"Mum," I called down the stairs, guessing that she would already be baking for the day. She came rushing up the stairs, flour all over her hands and apron. "What is it? Where's the fire?" she asked.

I couldn't get my words out. Colin came out with a shower cap on and a towel around his waist.

"Sorry Aurora," he said. "Force of habit. I'll be more careful to lock the door from now on."

"Thank you," I smiled grimly, trying to push the image of Colin's wobbly body out of my mind.

Mum looked from me to Colin and burst out

laughing. "Colin," she said, her voice husky. "Are you being naughty?" She pulled him closer and nibbled his ear.

"Give over woman," he joked. "I have to get dressed." Mum wiped flour off him, laughed and slapped him on the bottom. He gave her a cheeky grin before walking away to their bedroom.

Ugh! This was far too much to handle this early in the morning.

Mum turned back to me with an unashamed expression.

I hurried into the bathroom, washed, dressed and had breakfast. Wholewheat toast and boiled eggs at Mum's insistence.

Afterwards, I thought I would go for a drive to try to clear my head. I took the front entrance out of the flat, hoping that Mum wouldn't see me. No such luck. There she was, outside the café, writing out the breakfast deals on the menu with chalk.

"And just where might you be going?" she asked, raising her eyebrows at me.

"I might pop out for a bit," I shrugged.

"Well, don't be too long. I thought we might do a bit of shopping later."

"Shopping?" I asked. "What for?"

"Well," she said. "In case it's escaped your attention, it's almost Christmas and I'm going to have my first grandchild. I would like to buy some gifts." She paused, casting a critical eye over my outfit. "While we are there, I really think that you should get yourself some new clothes."

I looked at my outfit and back to her. "New clothes? Whatever for? I'm nearly nine months pregnant. Leggings and jumpers are just fine for me."

She shrugged her shoulders as if I was being tiresome. "I'm just saying, you ought to smarten yourself up. You're never going to get Nick back looking like that."

"Who said I wanted Nick back? Mother, I will see you later," I said, trying to brush off her comment and kissing her on the cheek.

"Make sure that you're back by lunchtime," she called after me. "Colin can cover for me."

"Fine," I said. I got into the car and checked my watch, only nine o'clock. Where was I going to go this early in the morning? I wondered about Rachel's invitation to come over. She'd probably have her hands full sorting out the children this early. I decided to drive to the seafront for a bit before asking her if I could come over.

I pulled up in the car park and got a takeaway decaf tea from the kiosk that I was surprised to see was still here after all these years. I sat down on a bench watching the restless waves. Only a few people were about, mainly dog walkers milling around with their dogs.

A memory of Michael Morday and I came to mind. Hand in hand, strolling along the sand on one of our late-night meetings. The beach was our special place that we'd sneak out of the house and come to, to be alone together. We'd spend hours here talking about the future. Everything was so certain back then. We promised each other we would never break-up, marry and have a bunch of children. How quickly all of those promises turned to dust.

I forced the thought from my mind. All that belonged to yesterday. No point in dwelling. Yet Michael lingered in my mind as I text Rachel: *Fancy a visitor?*

To my delight, she instantly texted back to say she would love one and was looking forward to

33

seeing me.

Rachel answered the door with a harassed expression and a bawling toddler on her hip. "Aurora," she said. "How are you love?"

"Surviving at Mum's. Have I come at a bad time?"

She sighed. "It's never a good time."

"Hello, Maisie," I said. She stopped crying for a moment and regarded me as if to say, do I know you? But quickly started up crying again, as if she got bored with guessing.

"Oh," Rachel said, glancing at the little one. "She's fine – been like this off and on all morning. It's the terrible two's and I think that she's tired. Come in."

"Aww," I said, stepping inside. "The joys of parenthood, eh?"

"Something like that. Fancy a bacon sandwich?" she asked.

"I'd love one," I said, picking my way around toys on the floor and following her into the kitchen.

I sat down on a seat at the kitchen island. "Can you hold her a sec?" Rachel asked, plonking Maisie on my lap before I could answer. "Her sister's asleep but with the racket she's making I'm surprised."

I spotted a baby book on the table and read it to Maisie, doing all the farmyard noises while Rachel fried the bacon and buttered some bread. To my surprise, she stopped crying and started joining in.

"You've got a knack with her," Rachel noted.

I laughed.

"No, really, I mean it," she said, taking Maisie from me and putting her in her highchair. She peeled and chopped a banana and gave it to her to munch on.

I smiled, wondering if she was just saying that to be kind. I wasn't used to being around small children. I had no idea how to look after a child but I'd have to learn quickly. Mum would no doubt want to be supportive, but with her being so bossy, I wondered how long I'd manage to stick living at home. And with Mum and Colin being so loved up, I felt like an intruder in the flat.

Rachel set two steaming mugs of decaf tea in front of us and glanced at me quizzically. "You look like you've got something on your mind, Aurora?"

She brought over our bacon sandwiches and sat down beside me. I sighed and offloaded to her about finding things difficult with Mum and unexpectedly meeting Colin.

Rachel smiled. "She never changes, does she? She always was overprotective and bossy. Don't you think that it's nice that she has a boyfriend though?"

"Yeah, I would if they weren't carrying on like a

couple of lovesick teenagers."

Rachel's expression turned sad. "Darren and I were like that once, not that I can remember it," she said, with a faraway glance.

"Everything alright with you two?" I asked her.

"Yeah," she said. "It's just hard to keep the romance alive when you have two small children."

"I can imagine," I said, hugging my hands around my mug. "Sorry that I didn't keep in touch – you know, after I left."

She shrugged. "I didn't expect that you would – I mean I always thought that you'd be much too busy with your own life."

"I know, but I wish I had made more of an

effort."

She put down her tea and wrapped her arms around my shoulders. "Never mind, you're back now." A high-pitched wail came from another room. "Honestly," she said, "If it's not one, then it's the other."

She brought Rosie through and set her up in her highchair, before heating up a jar of baby food. She tested it with a finger before she fed it to her. Then she cleaned up the mess Maisie had made, getting more banana on her face than in her mouth.

When I had finished, she cleared away the plates into the sink. "I didn't like to say yesterday, what with your mum there and everything, I think you're better off without that idiot Nick. It sounds like he really loves himself."

She didn't know the half of it. "Yes, I am, I know I am, it's just that it's hard. I didn't plan on bringing up this child alone."

She turned back to me. "Well, you're not alone, you've got me and your mum."

"Speaking of Mum," I said, checking my watch. "I'd better get going before she calls to see where I am."

"You know where I am if you need me love," Rachel said, hugging me. "Let's have a girlie night soon, like we used to, with face packs and a good rom-com."

"Sounds like bliss," I said and drove back to

the café, feeling a little brighter. Then I saw

Mum, standing with her arms folded outside

the café. She eyed me with a grumpy

expression, and I felt my good mood already

fading.

Chapter Four

"I've been waiting for ages, I was beginning to think that you had forgotten," Mum grumbled as she got into the car.

"Sorry," I said, trying to keep my tone even. "I went to see Rachel."

"Well, let's get going before we hit rush hour traffic."

I put my foot down and stared out the window. I would have liked to say the drive to our nearest town, Evergreen was a pleasant one, but with Mum tutting at my driving and my choice of music, my nerves were shredded by the time that we reached Charrington's. *It was exactly as I remembered it,* a little department store, a relic of its art deco glory days. Inside the store, the Christmas music boomed out and trees with glitzy lights were at every turn. Vague memories came back to me of seeing Santa and buying soft toys in the toy department.

"Right," Mum said, interrupting my thoughts. "First things first, you definitely need some new clothes."

She was already dragging me to the maternity section in womenswear before I could protest. "Look at this," she said, holding up a daisy patterned dress. "They do some lovely things for pregnant ladies."

"I don't really think that's me," I said. It was

more her style than mine. "I really don't need any new clothes."

She shook her head as if she disagreed and moved on to another patterned dress.

"How, about this?" I asked, swiftly picking up a denim dress and a pair of jeans. They would do for after the birth while I still had the baby weight.

"Fine," she said. "Anything has got to be better than what you're wearing."

I bit my lip, wondering how long I could stop myself from snapping back at her. Half an hour later, we had moved onto the baby section and my patience was waning. Mum kept picking out expensive sleepsuits that were overpriced. I said no to all of them bar one with little yellow teddies on. That would do for a special occasion.

"How about this?" she said, picking up a little pink and white striped dress.

"I don't even know that I'm having a girl yet," I said, thinking it was hideous.

She rolled her eyes at me. "Oh Aurora, why didn't you find out what the sex of the baby was? It would make your life so much easier."

"Nick and I decided we wanted it to be a surprise."

"Well," she muttered. "It's not what I would have done."

"Well, it's what I did," I said, through gritted

teeth. We moved onto the sale section and stocked up on a few essential items. Then Mum suggested that we head to the restaurant on the third floor.

"Shouldn't we be heading back home?" I asked. "What about Colin?"

"Don't worry about him," she said. "I'm sure everything's under control."

In the café, we joined a long queue and I took off my coat, feeling hot and uncomfortable.

Finally, we reached the counter. "What will you have?" Mum asked.

I looked at the food on display, trays of cottage pie, lasagne and macaroni cheese. "I'll have gravy, pie and chips," I said.

Mum raised her eyebrows. "That's hardly going to be healthy for the baby, is it?"

"It's what I fancy," I snapped.

The woman behind the counter gave me a sympathetic stare. "When I was pregnant with my daughter, I loved cucumber sandwiches."

"Really?" I said, politely. "Well, I love nothing more than chips - especially with pie," I added, enjoying Mum's disgruntled expression.

Mum ordered a tuna jacket potato and we moved on to the till with an array of cakes in front of it. "Look at those cakes," she muttered, eyeing up a plate of chocolate cupcakes with snowmen and reindeer faces on. "They must have been on display for days. I would never do that."

I blushed as the till assistant gave us a frosty look. Mum took no notice.

We sat down with our meals and ate in stony silence for a bit. My phone started buzzing from inside my bag.

Mum raised an eyebrow. "Well, aren't you going to answer it?"

I pulled the phone out of my bag and stared at the name of the caller, *Nick*. What on earth did he want?

"Who's that?" she asked, peering over my shoulder.

"Nothing - no one," I said, putting the phone on the table where it continued to buzz and vibrate. A foolish mistake I quickly realised, when Mum picked it up.

"Nick, I see. Well, aren't you going to answer it?"

"Just leave it," I said, snatching the phone and shoving it back in my bag. He would probably be calling about something trivial, like one of his possessions he thought I still had. He rarely asked about the baby.

"Oh, there's Paula, my Yoga teacher," Mum said. I followed her gaze to a stick-thin woman in a red coat and black scarf getting cutlery.

"I didn't know you did Yoga, Mum," I said.

"There's a lot you don't know, Aurora."

I didn't want to get into another argument with

her, so I ignored her comment.

Mum almost wrenched her arm out of its socket to wave to Paula. "Cooee. Cooee," she called to her.

Paula waved back and walked towards us with her head bent down. She looked just as embarrassed as I felt.

I turned to Paula as she came to the table with as much of a smile as I could muster.

"Paula," Mum said. "This is my daughter Aurora. I told you she's pregnant."

I laughed awkwardly as Paula bent down and put a hand on my stomach.

"Oh, I can feel the baby," Paula cried excitedly. My eyes widened and she took her hand away. "You should come to my pregnant Pilates class Aurora. You look like you could benefit," Paula said. Mum nodded in agreement.

"Yes, I will try," I said to be polite, thinking she was rude. Anyway, you wouldn't drag me kicking and screaming. *A walk was an effort never mind a stretching class.*

"You know Mum," I said. "I really need to go to the bathroom."

"I'll come with you," Mum said, already grabbing her handbag.

"There really is no need. Why don't you finish your chat and meet me up at the women's lingerie section?"

"Fine," she said. Although she didn't look like it was.

After nipping to the toilet, I wandered the women's lingerie section and scoured the nursing bras. I found two I liked and dithered over whether to buy one in baby blue or candy pink.

Buying both seemed like an extravagance. I glanced across the aisles in case Mum should approach and instead spotted Michael Morday, perusing women's pyjamas. I smiled as he fought to put back a flannel-checked pair of pyjamas on an overflowing rack. I wondered if I should go over and say hello, or just ditch the bras and run – well, waddle away.

Hang on a minute, what was he doing looking

at women's PJs? Nothing about a girlfriend on his social media account and I had looked once or twice. Alright, a few times... hmm... maybe he had a new girlfriend and hadn't got round to changing his status.

Come on Aurora, what does it matter? Just get out of there fast and avoid the whole awkward hug thing and how have you been malarky. He turned and started walking straight towards me.

My heart quickened in my chest and what happened next – well, I shouldn't have done it. No, as a thirtysomething-year-old woman I should have been more grown-up and said how great it was to see him again or something. Instead, I ducked behind a mannequin wearing pink silk PJs.

"Aurora, is that you?" he asked, peering over the mannequin at me like I was a stray cat.

Busted. "Oh, yes, it's me," I said, groaning with the effort of getting up again. I accidently knocked the mannequin's arm out of its socket. "Surprise," I cried, trying to put it back in place. It wouldn't work and I was getting eyed by a staff member so I left it dangling.

"Aurora?" he asked, looking at me curiously. "Were you hiding from me?"

"Erm...no, not exactly," I said.

"Well," he said, clearing his throat. "I'm glad to see you, I heard that you were back in town."

So awkward. "Yes." *Three guesses which little*

bird told him that…

His gorgeous green eyes drifted to my stomach. "Wow. You're really pregnant now."

"Yes, I know," I said, pointing to my stomach. "A beached whale."

"No," he said with a gleam in his eye. "No, I wasn't thinking that." He blushed and quickly changed the subject. "Home just for the holidays or are you moving back? What's his name not with you?"

"Nick, no, we're getting a divorce."

"Really?" he asked. From the genuine look of surprise on his face, maybe Mum hadn't told him, but surely, he must have heard it from someone in town or *Stars* magazine.

He saw me looking at him curiously. "Well, I mean that is just awful. I'm sorry," he added, with a serious expression.

"Yes, well it's probably for the best and to answer your other question, I'm not moving back to Green Leaf permanently. Just until I have the baby and then I'm going to figure things out. Don't you have a girlfriend?"

"Nope, no girlfriend," he grinned.

"That's a shame. You're too busy running the bookshop I expect."

"Yes, I guess," he said. His eyes met mine. Was there regret and longing in his eyes? Or was I just imagining things? Probably the latter.

"Well," he said. "We must catch up soon. I'd

better get on. I'm shopping for my sister."

"That explains the ladies pyjamas," I laughed, now my turn to blush. *Great, now he'll think I'm a stalker!*

We hugged and I watched him walk away, half wishing I was a teenager again.

"There you are."

"Mum," I said, almost jumping out of my skin. "Do you have to creep up on me?"

"Sorry." She glanced behind me to Michael going for the down escalator. "Is that Michael Morday?"

"Yes." *Trust her to miss nothing.*

"Well, I hope you're not thinking about letting

him back in your life, are you? No point in raking over old ghosts, is there?"

I was about to tell her it was none of her business when she asked, "You're getting those nursing bras, I take it then?"

I glanced down at the nursing bras, still dangling limply in my hand. No wonder Michael couldn't get away fast enough.

Chapter Five

Mrs Nelson, daily café visitor, held up the front page of *Stars* magazine to me. "Have you seen this?" she asked.

I stopped clearing up plates and glanced up at the headline: *Splitsville for Nick Hope and top model Amanda Jensen. A* picture of Nick looking disheveled and his six-foot-something, legs up to her armpits, Swedish supermodel girlfriend with dark sunglasses on. A big thunderbolt between them.

I shrugged, feeling numb. "Doesn't really surprise me, he's probably already onto someone else."

Mrs Nelson's jaw dropped and she held the cover up to Mum. "You've seen this?"

Mum cleared her throat and glared at her. "Yes, I have."

"I'm going on a break now," I said, not wanting to talk about it anymore.

I checked my phone in the flat kitchen. Five missed calls from Nick. I had never had so many calls in a day from him. Ever. It didn't take a genius to work out he was calling for sympathy. Well, if he thought he was going to boomerang back to me, he had another thing coming.

I started a message to him and typed: *What do you want?* My finger hovered over the send button when Mother came upstairs. "Nick's been calling you again I take it?" she said, glancing at my phone. "Now he isn't with Amanda, I hope you will at least hear him out."

"Mum, will you stay out of it, please?"

"Look, a text won't be any good," she pressed on. "Why don't you call him?"

"Fine," I said, deleting the text. "I'll phone him when I have time."

Patricia's voice boomed up the stairs. "Look, I don't know what's going on between you two but if table two doesn't get their hot chocolates and coffee and walnut cake there's going to be hell on."

Mum raised her eyebrows. "I'll go down and

sort it out Aurora. Why don't you make that phone call?"

I sighed as Colin came into the kitchen. He took one look at the pained expression on my face, made me a cup of tea and left. Unlike Mum, he had quickly developed a knack of knowing when I needed some space.

I sat down, stirring sugar into my tea. I supposed that I'd better try Nick's number otherwise I'd get no peace. I dialed the number hoping that he wouldn't answer. He did. On the first ring.

"Aurora," he said, his voice still as smooth and charming as ever.

"Look, Nick, I'm really busy helping Mum in the

café," I said, not wanting this conversation to go on longer than was necessary. "Why do you keep calling me? What do you want?"

"You've been working in the café?" he asked, his voice rising. "You shouldn't be doing that when you're so near your time to give birth. You should be resting now; not running around."

"I'm fine," I insisted. Well, other than the fact that my ankles looked like Christmas puddings and my stomach would barely fit behind the till. I felt better than I had done in weeks. "What's it to you, anyway?"

"I'm just worried about you, that's all. Look - I've been thinking, I should come up to Green Leaf."

My stomach lurched. "I don't want you here." I hadn't planned on having him at the birth and he hadn't even been to any of the scans. I was going to do this on my own, and that was just fine.

"Just think about it," he said, undeterred. "You'll need someone there with you when the time comes."

"I'm fine, I've got Mum," I insisted, my voice wobbling.

"I want to be there, if you'll let me. We're in this together."

He'd changed his tune. "I've got to go," I said, tears pricking at my eyes.

"Aurora, just think about it, will you?"

I switched the phone off and wiped the tears away, hating the way that he thought he could just waltz back into my life when he felt like it.

I took a few deep breaths, swallowed down a glass of water and went back downstairs. Mum was busy pouring coffee beans into the cappuccino machine.

"Well," she said, glancing up at me. "I can tell from your face it didn't go well."

"Just leave it will you," I said, "I'm in no mood to talk." I walked away to start clearing up tables, hoping that she would just drop it. She didn't, she followed me and tried to help. "Honestly Aurora, sometimes you're your own worst enemy."

"Mum," I said, looking her straight in the eye. "I'm done talking about this."

"All I'm saying is that he is the father of your child. At least try and talk to him. Maybe he's genuinely sorry."

"You don't have a clue what you're talking about," I shouted and went quiet, realising that the Tuesday knitting group had stopped mid-stitch. They peered at us over coffee and yule log. I turned and went through the swing door into the kitchen and began stacking the dishwasher.

"Aurora," Mum called through the door with a frosty glare.

"What now, Mum?" I asked, wiping fresh tears

away.

"You can't bury your head in the sand forever. The baby will be here in a matter of days. You're going to need support."

I scowled at her. "Look, in case you've forgotten, he was the one who left me and said that he wanted nothing to do with me or the baby. I can't just let him back into our lives to walk out again. Can I? Anyway, I don't know why you're so bothered. My father, wasn't there at my birth, was he?" I trailed off, knowing I had overstepped it.

We never mentioned my father. Not since the day I proudly told everyone at school my father was in the navy and had died at sea. I thought he was a hero until the school bully laughed in my face and told me it was a lie.

I ran home to ask Mum about it, but she told me that the bully was the liar and not her. I knew though as children do, when an adult is lying. Not being able to bear the pain etched on her face, I never brought it up again. Until now.

Mum's smile tightened, and she forced back the tears from her eyes. "I've told you before, Aurora. Your father was away at sea when you were born and his ship got sunk by an enemy aircraft, he drowned."

I shook my head in disbelief, even now she was sticking to that fairy-tale. "I can't believe you're still lying, after all this time."

She opened her mouth to speak, but I

interrupted her. "You don't want to tell me the truth. I get it. It hurt me when I was younger but I won't let it now. Anyway, you managed to bring me up on your own, didn't you, without my father? You managed, didn't you?"

Mum sighed and came over to help. "Because I had to, Aurora. If Nick is offering you some help, then don't you think you should take it?"

"Mother, please, plenty of women have babies without men in their lives. It's the 21st century."

"Hmm..." she said, her eyes full of criticism.

I was grateful when the café front doorbell jangled. A customer, something to distract us from this argument.

Both of us went out to the front to see who it

was.

"Michael," I said, surprised.

"Aurora," he said, looking at my apron. "I see your mum's keeping you busy."

"Yes," I said, narrowing my eyes at Mum. Her eyes were burning into my back.

"Michael," she said with a false smile. "Can I help you with anything?"

"Well, I was coming in for a piece of your turkey pie."

"One slice of pie coming right up," she said, getting a pie dish from the display counter.

I took my apron off. "I was just going to go out for a walk Michael," I said. I wanted to get away from the café for a bit and I secretly hoped he'd come with me.

"I can walk with you if you like?" he smiled.

"I wouldn't want to spoil your lunch," I said. Mum had already cut him a big slice of pie.

"Oh, you wouldn't be and anyway, I rather fancy fish and chips now, if you're up for it?"

"What about your pie?" Mum asked.

"Wrap it up and I'll have it later."

Mum put the pie in a brown paper bag. "That'll be £3.60, please," she said.

Michael handed over a fiver and Mum rung it through the till.

"I'll be with you in a second, I'll just grab my

coat," I said, already opening the side door and disappearing up the stairs before Mum could say anything about it.

"Aurora," Mum called after me. "Don't have too many chips."

I ignored her and retrieved my thick fleecy parka.

When I came back downstairs, she eyeballed me like she wanted to say something.

"I'll see you in a bit," I said to her, following Michael out of the café, before she could say anymore. I'd had enough of talking about my father and Nick.

Michael and I fell into step and walked a little way through the narrow high street towards the fish shop. Suddenly, he stopped and turned to me.

"So, are you going to tell me what's wrong? You seemed to be in quite a hurry to get out."

"Nothing's wrong." He looked at me like he didn't believe me. "It's just Mother sticking her big size sixes in about Nick," I explained. "He wants to come up here and be there at the birth."

"I see. I take it you don't want that, well it's your choice." A serious look came over his face. "Who are you going to have with you at the birth?"

"Mother, that's if we don't kill each other first."

"I'll be your birthing partner if you like - I mean,

I don't want you to go through it alone."

"Thank you," I said. "It's sweet of you, but you hardly know me anymore. I can't ask you to do that."

"Well, it wouldn't bother me. We may have not seen each other for a while, but I still care about you." He turned to me with a sparkle in his eyes.

"Thanks," I said, touched by his kind gesture.

He insisted on paying for the fish and chips. When we came out of the shop, he turned to me and said, "It's a bit too chilly out here for a walk along the seafront, why don't we take them back to the bookshop? I'll make us a cup of tea."

"Sounds good," I said, and without thinking, I linked my arm through his, exactly the way I used to. I looked at him, wondering if he would shrug me off but he clung to my arm tighter.

Back in Green Sleeves, I gasped in horror when he switched the lights on. "You could do with some Christmas spirit around here," I said. Unlike The Leaves of Change Café, there was only a limp Christmas tree standing by the small reading corner. It had no decorations apart from a sparse helping of tinsel plonked on it.

He shrugged. "Maybe, I'm just not feeling in the Christmas mood."

"Really, why is that?"

His smile faded at my question. "No reason. The office is just back here." He led the way through to the back of the bookshop behind the counter.

I followed him, wondering why he didn't like Christmas. He had always loved it when we were together.

I glanced around at the cardboard boxes and piles of books to find a seat at his desk, or what he could use as one if he tidied up.

"Sorry about the mess," he said. "I wasn't expecting guests. There's normally just me, apart from a young university lad who comes in on a Saturday and the odd afternoon."

He took the fish and chips out of the bag and

cleared the desk while I hunted to find clean cups. None in the cupboard. Just two dirty cups on the draining board. I started cleaning them when he took them off me. His hands brushed against mine for a moment and a spark of electricity shot right the way through me. I tried to pretend it hadn't happened and filled up the kettle.

He took the kettle from me. "You sit yourself down and then I'll make us that cup of tea."

"Thanks," I said. I cleared the books from the chair and put them next to the overflowing pile on the floor. "You must love working here and being able to read books all day. Sounds like heaven."

He turned to me with a wide smile. "Well,

you'd think that, wouldn't you, but I never seem to stop. If I'm not sorting out new stock, I'm doing the accounts or chasing up orders. It can be a lot."

He set the two teas down on the desk and gave me my fish and chips. I wondered where he would sit until he dragged a stool from the corner and sat on it beside me.

"It's funny how we both ended up back here," I said, stabbing my chips with a wooden fork. "I always thought you wanted to be a writer and live in Paris."

He chuckled, taking a bite of fish. "Somehow, I ended up as a banker working in London, but to tell you the truth, I couldn't stand the rat race. I saw this place was up for sale and bought it, quit my job and came up here."

"Just like that?" I asked, thinking it all seemed so sudden.

He looked away. "Yes, well, there were other reasons, but it's worked out for me pretty well so far. What about you? You're a big actress now? Eh?"

"Hardly," I laughed. "I took classes after Uni, that's where I met Nick. He became a runaway success. I tried for a bit but I couldn't get anything bigger than the odd commercial."

"Yes," he said. "I think I remember you in the advert for washing powder. You played a mum."

"Yes, the highlight of my career." I laughed

and looked down at my bump. "I suppose it was good practice."

He smiled, creasing the dimples in his cheeks. "You know I've thought about you a lot over the years. I wish things hadn't ended the way they did. I should never have – well, I shouldn't have dumped you for Melissa Clarke. It was just that I was so messed up about you going away and we were arguing a lot."

Melissa Clarke - the reason for our break up. The mention of her name still gave me a pain in my chest but I wasn't going to tell him that. "Yes, well it was a long time ago. I wonder where she is now? Did you keep in touch?"

"Nope, it fizzled out not long after you left for Uni. She's probably married with a bunch of kids now."

"Probably," I agreed. "How come you never got married?"

"Well, no one could compare to my first love."

My heart leapt to my throat as he leaned in as if he was going to kiss me. Then his face erupted into a childlike grin.

"My first love - books, that is."

"Hilarious."

"No, seriously," he said, his eyes held that regretful look I had seen at Charrington's the other day. "I've thought about you a lot over the years. I wrote a letter to you but I never sent it."

"You did?" I asked, surprised. "I thought when

I didn't hear from you after our break-up, you were glad things were over."

He shook his head. "Aurora. I'm really sorry if I hurt you."

"Ah, it's all water under the bridge, isn't it?" I said, a lump rising in my throat. I swallowed it back down. "I should go."

His eyes traced my face with remorse. "Mother will be on the warpath again, sending out the café regulars to come and look for me." I paused, thinking I was silly to get so upset. Michael and me were a lifetime ago. Why shouldn't we be friends? I glanced around the office. "You really could do with some decorations around here."

"Why?" he asked. "What do you suggest?"

"You'll see," I grinned. "You'll see."

Chapter Six

That evening while Mum was at Yoga, I hunted out some extra Christmas decorations from the cupboard at the top of the stairs and caught sight of gold tinsel peeking out of a box.

"I thought I heard someone banging about," a gruff voice said.

I turned to see Colin, probably coming through to see what all the fuss was about. "Here Aurora, let me give you a hand," he said, reaching for the box. "You shouldn't be lifting things in your condition."

"Thanks," I said. He got out the box with the gold tinsel in it for me and another behind it marked: *Old Xmassy decorations.*

I followed him into the living room where he set the boxes on the floor. Both of us started having a good rummage inside.

Some decorations were actually quite tasteful, surprising for Mum, hanging animal ornaments, sparkly bows, reindeer, baubles and massive amounts of tinsel.

We had decided on a few that would be useable in Green Sleeves, when I heard the front door open. Mum came dashing up the stairs and appeared in her workout gear and headband.

"What on earth do you want with those old things?" she asked, looking at the piles of decorations on the floor.

"Oh, nothing, I'm just helping a friend out."

Up went the raised eyebrows again. "By friend I take it you mean Michael? Doesn't he have his own Christmas decorations?"

I took out a couple of hanging bear ornaments, dressed in red and green waistcoats. Somehow, they had remained hidden at the bottom.

"I'll put the kettle on, shall I?" Colin asked, obviously sensing there was an argument brewing.

"Yes, that would be great," Mum said, giving him a big kiss.

Colin disappeared out of the room. "Actually

Mum," I said, "not that it's any of your business, but they are for Michael."

"Hmm," I thought you were going to stay away from him, Aurora? He's already hurt you once, I don't want to see him do it again. And I take it you haven't spared a thought for Nick."

"Look, Mum, Nick doesn't fit into my plans. I'm having this baby by myself whether you like it or not."

"You're too stubborn for your own good, Aurora."

I rolled my eyes at her as Colin came back in with the coffees, decaf for me. "Everything alright in here?" he asked.

"Fine," Mum and I said in unison, a horrible

lump rose up in my throat.

"Right, great," he said, taking in the icy looks Mum and I were giving each other. He set the coffees down and helped me untangle some fairy lights.

"I've got something to do in the café." Mum shrugged, taking her coffee and heading downstairs.

I bit back the tears that were threatening to fall and wished I hadn't let Mum get me so upset.

"Aw, now," Colin said reading my face. "We can't have you upset, can we? I'll fetch us both a brownie and we can have a chat about it."

He returned with one on a plate for each of us.

"Here you go," he said, handing me mine. "Get

this down you." I took a big bite and the sugariness of the brownie gave me an instant lift.

"I don't know how you've managed to put up with Mum for so long, Colin," I said.

"Aww, she's a pussy cat underneath," he said, taking a sip of coffee.

"Not to me. If she's not going on about me and Nick getting back together, she's criticising me for spending time with Michael."

Colin smiled with sympathy in his eyes. "You know your mother. She's a bossy boots but her heart's in the right place."

"I know," I sighed. "I just wish she could see things from my point of view."

"She'll come round."

"I hope so," I said. "Otherwise, I'll have to find somewhere else to live."

Colin sucked in his breath between his teeth. "It wouldn't come to that, surely?"

I shrugged. "I really hope not, but I don't know if I can take much more of her interfering in my life."

I kept myself awake that night checking the housing market on my phone, looking for places to let nearby. There weren't many. Most of the people in this town had lived here for years. They had brought up children here and stayed for their retirement.

The ones that were available were out of my

price range. I couldn't afford to move back to London either, not that I really wanted to. Just as well, even the prices of the smallest apartments made my eyes water. I could have asked Nick for money, but I didn't want to be beholden to him. Nope, like or lump it, I was stuck here.

Chapter Seven

Mid-afternoon in the café the following day and most of the regulars had already been and gone. I asked Mum if she wouldn't mind if I popped out for a bit.

"I suppose you're going to the bookshop," she said. "I can't stop you but you know what I think. Don't be too late, I'll need some help with clearing up."

Colin appeared, carrying the decorations we had sorted the previous evening.

"Ready to go?" he asked.

"I'll just grab my coat."

I saw Mum eyeing the box and hurried out through the door to the flat.

At Green Sleeves, Colin placed the box on the end of the counter. I began picking out tinsel and ornaments from it.

Michael glanced up from bagging a book for a customer. "Are all these for me?"

"Well," I said, glancing at the limp tree in the reading corner. "On one condition. That thing has definitely got to go."

"Deal," Michael agreed and all three of us laughed.

"It's a good job that I know just the place that sells Christmas trees," Colin said.

"Great," I said. "I'll close up shop and make a

start on cleaning up if you two want to go and get one."

When they had both gone, I set to work dusting the counter and adding tinsel around it. In the office, I organised the paperwork into files and sorted out the kitchen area. After adding some tinsel around the notice board and a miniature tree in the centre of the table, I began putting books on the shelves.

When I got to the bottom shelf, I noticed a photograph sticking out underneath the bookcase. I reached for it and my stomach flipped when I realised that it was of Michael and a woman with beautiful auburn hair.

I judged from him not having that grey streak in his hair that the photograph was from a while ago. They stood outside the bookshop with their arms around each other and grins on their faces. The way her eyes seemed to sparkle as she looked at him… she must be some old girlfriend. I left it on the end of a shelf of books on the bookcase, trying to squash the pain in the pit of my stomach.

I continued tidying and decorating whilst wondering what the woman in the photograph was called and what had happened between them. Were they still in touch? Did he still have feelings for her?

I was so lost in thought that I didn't hear Michael and Colin coming back.

"Wow," said Michael, glancing around the office and breaking my thoughts. "I've never seen the place looking so tidy. You should come and see the Christmas tree, Colin got it at half price."

"Well, it helps when you're the boss," Colin chuckled.

"You own a garden centre, Colin?" I asked, surprised. Mum had mentioned that he owned a store but I had obviously been caught up in my own problems to pay much attention.

"Yes," he said. "But I have an excellent manager running it for me, I just pop back there every now and again to check up on the place."

"Well, let's see this tree," I said and followed them both out to the shop front where a huge fir tree sat on its side, stretching halfway across the bookshop.

"Well, do you like it?" Michael asked.

"Yes, it's very impressive, but it'll be a tight squeeze to fit it into the reading corner though."

"I'm sure that we'll manage," Michael said.

Colin and Michael set up the tree while I made us all a much-needed cup of tea.

"It looks alright, doesn't it?" Michael asked when I returned, cups in hand.

"Yeah," I agreed, stepping back and staring at the giant tree. "I'm sure it'll look great when we get some decorations on it."

"Well, I'll leave that up to both of you and get

back to the café to help your mum clear up," Colin said.

"Thank you, Colin," I said.

Michael and I set to work, decorating the tree with all the tinsel, baubles and fairy lights I had brought.

"There," I said, standing back from all our hard work when we had finished. "Well, what do you think?"

Michael glanced at me with a smile that reached his eyes. "It's perfect now."

"Well, not quite," I pondered, my eyes on the empty space underneath the bottom branches. "There is something missing. No tree is complete without presents, and I have the perfect idea. Why don't we wrap up books and put them under the tree? You could have a mystery book giveaway, free entry with every book sold. The winners would be drawn just before Christmas."

"Great idea," he said. "Let me help you choose some books."

I chose a couple of children's Christmas books, some romantic and crime fiction, and he chose some science fiction and classics. We sat together in the office side by side with some Christmas music on. I wrapped up the books and he tied the ribbons around them when I'd finished.

"You know, when I was cleaning up," I began tentatively. "I found a photograph of you and a woman."

"Oh, where?" he asked, he sounded casual but I caught the pain in his eyes.

"It's on the bookshelf," I said, pointing to the end of a stack of books. He got up as if I'd forced him to. His face darkened as he picked up the photograph and stared at it for a moment. I was sorry that I had brought the subject up.

"I didn't mean to upset you," I said, almost wishing I hadn't mentioned it.

"You didn't," he said, putting the photograph in the bin. "It's just that I don't like to talk about it."

"I understand," I said. However, much as I wished he'd open up to me, I didn't want to push him. Still, all the unanswered questions about this mysterious woman circled in my mind.

Chapter Eight

Every time that the café bell jangled, I glanced up to see if it was Michael. When it wasn't, I wondered if he was avoiding me, in case I asked him more questions about the woman in the photograph. I stood at the counter, my mobile in my hand, thinking about texting him but not knowing what to say. At least Nick hadn't bothered me again. I hoped that he had given up his idea of coming to Green Leaf.

Mum came over to the counter. "Aurora, snap out of it please, there are customers to serve."

"Yes, sorry Miss Wilson," I said, turning to the customer, clad in tartan from head to toe, her snappy terrier in her arms. "Your usual? Teacake and hot chocolate?"

"Yes," she smiled. "You looked away with the fairies then. Were you thinking about the baby?"

"Yes," I said, turning to fetch the cocoa powder. She took one of the free dog biscuits from the counter and shuffled into a seat in the corner.

"Aurora, can I have a quick word please?" I turned to see Michael standing there with a worried expression on his face.

"Yes," I said, my stomach churning with worry. I hoped that he wasn't going to say he didn't think we should spend any more time together.

It was almost all I had looked forward to lately.

Mum put her hand on her hip. "Anything you've got to say, you can say in front of me."

"Mum, it's fine, really," I said and turned to Michael. "Shall we pop upstairs for a minute?"

"I'll finish Miss Wilson's order then, shall I?" Mum asked.

I nodded.

"I'm right here if you need anything," she mouthed as Michael and I went up the stairs.

In the kitchen, I poured out a glass of water for us both and we sat down at the table.

"I'm sorry about the other day," he said. "I didn't mean to be off-hand with you. It's just that seeing that photograph again stirred up uncomfortable memories for me."

I stretched out my hand to his. "It's okay, you don't have to tell me."

He sighed heavily. "No, I want to. That photograph you found was of Michelle, my ex-fiancée. It was a whirlwind romance. I met her in the summer a few years back when she was on holiday here and persuaded her to stay with me. We started running the bookshop together but she left me on Christmas Eve... before I even woke up."

He shook his head and swallowed hard at the memory. "She left me a note by the bed to say that she had been offered a job and was moving back to London. That Christmas I took all the decorations down and stayed in bed. I should have seen it coming, as she would never let me put anything about our relationship on social media or visit my sister. That should have told me she wasn't serious about us."

"I'm sorry," I said, squeezing his hand. "But maybe she wasn't the one."

His eyes gleamed at me. "No, I guess not. She's married to an old boyfriend now. That's why-□

"That's why you don't like Christmas," I interrupted.

"No, old wounds, I guess. But I did some thinking the other day. You being back, it's made me realise my feelings for you - I think there's still something between us?"

"I do too, it's just -" I paused and looked down at my bump.

"Bad timing?" he asked. "Friends?"

I squeezed his hand tighter. "Definitely."

"Do you want to see *Scrooge* with me on Saturday? It's at the local community centre, nothing special. It's not a date or anything. I just have some spare tickets, that's all."

"Yes, if I haven't gone into labour by then," I laughed, realising Saturday was the 21st of December. I was expecting the baby on Christmas Eve and I don't know why but I thought it might come early.

"Well, if you do, let me know – I meant what I said about being at the birth with you."

"Thank you," I said as he kissed me on the cheek.

I told myself that I had done the right thing – I had enough to worry about without starting something between us and I had to focus on the baby. Yet I couldn't deny the butterflies in my stomach when he looked at me or the heat that went through me at his touch.

Chapter Nine

"You've brightened up," Mum noted as we cleaned tables at the end of the day. "I don't suppose that it has anything to do with seeing Michael earlier?"

"No, I'm just in a good mood," I said, a little defensively.

"I don't know," she persisted, looking suspicious. "You've got that sparkle in your eye. I hope you're not falling for him again."

I shook my head as my phone buzzed and smiled at the text.

Rachel: Are you free tonight? For a girly night at mine?

Me: Why not?

Rachel: Eight o'clock. Alcohol free Margaritas?

Me: Can't wait. I texted her back and caught Mum peering over my shoulder. "I'm going out later to see Rachel," I said and put the phone back into my pocket.

Mum shook her head. "Honestly, I don't know where you get your energy. When I was pregnant with you, the only thing I felt like doing after a full day of work in the café was to go to bed."

I laughed. "I'm fine, really."

"You might laugh now," she said. "Just wait until the baby's born and you're rushed off your feet. You'll wish you'd rested."

"I like to be busy," I said, smiling at my bump.

I changed into the maternity jeans I had bought from my trip with Mum and a top that just went over my bump. The baby gave a kick and I patted my stomach gently. "Can't wait to meet you."

I picked up my bag and headed over to Rachel's. She greeted me with a face pack on and led the way into the living room. We sat down and she handed me a margarita.

"Don't worry, yours has no booze in it," she said.

"Can't quite say the same about mine, though," she added with a giggle. "Tonight, my house is a child-free zone. They're having a sleepover at their grandma's and Darren is at work, so we have the whole place to ourselves."

"Perfect."

"Right," she said. "I've got the pizza ordered, Bolognese still your favourite?"

"Yes," I said, glancing at the coffee table, covered with an assortment of 90's rom-coms. "Now this takes me back. Except that back in the day, it was videos, not DVD's."

"I know, aren't we old?" she laughed.

"Not tonight," I smiled, clinking my glass with hers. "Tonight, we can relive our youth."

"Yes," she said, "Sometimes, I wish I could."

I put my glass down. "Come on, things aren't that bad, are they?"

"No, they aren't. I just get sick of being a grownup sometimes. So much responsibility. Anyway, enough of that. What movie do you fancy?"

"Shall we put this one on?" I asked, holding up a movie we'd seen a hundred times.

"Face pack first," she grinned and fetched a bowlful of mixture that smelled like a combination of porridge oats and honey. It did the trick though; when she took it off, my skin felt much softer.

The pizza arrived, and we settled down to the DVD. It got to the part where the couple admit their true feelings when my phone buzzed. A text from Michael: *Still on for Saturday?*

Perfect. I texted back, a trill of excitement rushing through me.

Michael: *Pick you up at Eight? For our non-date?*

Me: *Lol can't wait.*

"I know that look," she said, pausing the movie and looking at me curiously. "Who was that texting you? Was it Michael?"

I nodded, feeling myself blush.

She topped up my margarita. "Spill."

"Yes, we've been spending a bit of time together. I helped him decorate the bookshop, and he's offered to be there for me at the birth."

Her smile widened. "I can't believe he offered to do that; he must still have feelings for you."

"Not you too," I joked. "Mum's already been on my case, she's told me I should stay away from him."

"Well, you're both grownups now. You should be able to make your own decisions."

"Try telling her that," I smiled.

"Well, how do you feel about him? That's what really matters."

Gorgeous and caring, even more of a catch than when we were teenagers. I couldn't say what I really felt though. "Well, he's a nice man-," I began.

"You have feelings for him, don't you?"

"No, well, maybe a little bit. But it's hardly the right time and there's a lot of water under the bridge between the two of us."

"I wouldn't worry about all that," she giggled. "The most important thing is how you feel about each other. He'll love the baby, I'm sure. Are you going to see him again?"

"Well, we are going to the community centre to see *Scrooge* on Saturday, but it isn't a date."

"Doesn't sound like one," she laughed and downed the rest of her drink.

"Give me a break, will you?" I said, gently nudging her in the arm.

"What about Nick? Has he been in touch with

you?"

"Oh," I said, taking a sip of my drink. "Not for a few days thankfully, but before that he was bothering me, saying he wanted to come to Green Leaf and be there at the birth. I told him I didn't want him there and I hope he's accepted that."

She patted me on the hand. "If I was you, I would feel the same. What about when the baby's born? What if he wants contact with the baby?"

"I haven't really thought that far ahead," I admitted. "I'd always thought that he wouldn't be interested in having anything to do with us, but I wouldn't stop him from seeing the baby if he wants to."

"So, I guess you'll have to talk to him sooner rather than later?"

"I will," I said. "Once the baby's born." I hated to admit it, but I knew she was right. I would have to face my problems eventually, but for now, all I wanted to do was to escape into eating pizza and watching the rest of the movie.

Chapter Ten

On Saturday, after the café closed Mum insisted on a family dinner. We sat across the table eyeballing each other and saying little. Colin in the middle of us, grasping at small talk. I hurried down the mountain of lentil bake that Mum had made and then tried to find something to wear for tonight.

A lot of my things were still in storage, but I had brought with me my faithful red velvet stretchy dress. I put it on, added a dash of red lipstick and smoothed my hair down in front of the mirror. Mum knocked on my door. I glanced around her to see Colin behind her, smiling at me. Both of them were dressed like they were off somewhere posh. Mum had on a sparkly dress and Colin wore a smart suit and tie.

"Where are you two off to?" I asked. "Anywhere nice?"

"Just to the local community centre," Mum answered nonchalantly.

My mood sank. All day I had been looking forward to having a quiet night out and getting away from Mum for a bit.

She looked at my red velvet dress with a dismissive eye. "And where might you be going? Off out with Michael, I presume?"

"Actually," I said. "Michael's taking me to the local community centre."

"I don't think that would be such a good idea,"

Mum said. "I mean you look tired, why don't you stay in and put your feet up?"

"I'm fine," I insisted, wondering if she really was concerned about me or just wanted to stop me from seeing Michael.

Mum narrowed her eyes and shook her head at me.

"Look," Colin said. "I'm sure that Aurora is more than capable of making her own decisions."

"Thank you, Colin," I said, grateful for his intervention.

The doorbell went. I hurried to put on my leather jacket and picked up my clutch bag. "Don't worry about me, I'll be fine Mum. See you both there."

"Maybe we should go with you," Mum said. "Colin can drive us all."

"No, I'll see you at the community centre," I said, kissing her on the cheek and moving towards the door.

Michael had made quite the effort with a smart shirt and jeans. "Shall we go?" I asked, linking his arm through mine.

"Yes, you look beautiful," he said.

"Thank you," I said, feeling huge.

No sooner had we got in the car than Mum and Colin came beetling out. She glared at Michael and me before joining Colin in the car.

"Where are they off to looking so smart? They're not going to the community centre, are they?" Michael joked.

"Yes, I'm afraid that they are," I frowned.

"Well, that's okay as long as we don't have to sit next to them."

I hope not! Thankfully, I couldn't see them as we arrived. I spotted Rachel and Darren in the foyer and said a quick hello to them. Glad to see that they were having a night out together for a change.

"Hope you enjoy yourselves," Rachel said and glanced from me to Michael with a mischievous twinkle in her eye. I promised to call her later. Doubtless she'd want all the gossip.

Michael and I took our seats just as the lights had dimmed, when I heard, "Psst Aurora, Aurora."

"Mum," I whispered, glaring at her. "What on earth are you doing?"

"One moment darling," she said. She pushed her way along the row with Colin behind her and asked the couple beside us if they wouldn't mind swapping seats. They agreed reluctantly and shuffled out of their seats, shaking their heads at her. Mum and Colin plonked themselves down beside us. I shrank back into my seat, as did Michael.

"Sorry, I tried to stop her," Colin said, glancing apologetically at me.

"Colin," Mum scolded, giving him a frosty stare.

"They must think that we need chaperoning," Michael said, trying to make light of it.

"I'm so sorry," I whispered to him. "We can leave if you want?"

"No, it's fine, the more the merrier," he grinned.

"Want a bon-bon?" Mum asked, leaning over us and rustling a sweet wrapper.

"No, thanks," I grimaced, mentally thanking Mum for ruining the whole evening.

The show started and I felt like I was a teenager again, with Mum hovering over us. She seemed to offer us a sweet every twenty seconds and cleared her throat every time our arms brushed on the armrest of the seat.

As soon as it was over, Mum helped me up by the elbow. "Right, let's get you home."

"Actually," I said. "Michael's going to take me home."

Her face clouded over and I hoped she wouldn't start another argument.

"Come on, Catherine," Colin said before she could say something else. "Let's go home and leave the young things to their own devices."

"Right," she said, kissing me on the cheek and glaring at Michael. "I'll see you at home, don't be too long."

Colin winked at me and they disappeared out

ahead of us.

"Home?" Michael asked as we got in the car.

"I don't feel like going home just yet," I said, enjoying being alone with him.

"Well, do you fancy hot chocolate at my house?"

My smile grew wider. "Yes, I would like that."

We got into the car and he started driving a little way out of town to the border between Green Leaf and Evergreen. I glanced out the window as we arrived at a detached house next to a field. "Woodpark House," I smiled. "I remember this place well."

I already knew that his parents lived here and that from the local gossips, he had inherited their house after they died. But I didn't know the full story, he had been very private about that.

He smiled sadly and turned off the engine. When he looked at me, there were tears in his eyes. "No, you see, buying the bookshop wasn't the only reason I came back."

"When I was working in London, my father died. I had been so busy with my job that I didn't make time to come home. Not long after that, my mother got sick. By then my sister had moved to Scotland. She had a family of her own and found it hard to commute. So, I quit my job, came home and took care of her until she passed. I bought the bookshop after that. Sorry I didn't quite tell you the truth – although

I'm sure you'll have heard what happened. It's just that it is another thing that's painful to talk about."

"I knew some of it," I said. "But I'm still glad that you've told me." I squeezed his hand, tears in my eyes. "I wish I could have been there for you and your mum."

His fingers interlocked with mine. "You weren't to know, were you? Anyway, glad you weren't there. Mum would want you to remember her the way she was, so full of life and not..." he trailed off and wiped the tears away.

I leaned across for a hug and closed my eyes, thinking that I could stay like this forever.

"Right," he said, breaking away from me.

"Shall we go in?"

We climbed out of the car and I eyed the tree filled with fairy lights in the window.

"I'm impressed," I said, holding his hand in mine. "I see someone's finally got their Christmas spirit."

He glanced at me with a sparkle in his eyes. "Well, I had a little help. Anyway, it's freezing, shall we go inside?"

He unlocked the door and to my delight, his living room was filled with Christmas cards dotted around the walls on a string. Gold and green tinsel hung around the fireplace and the walls. A proper log fire sat proudly in the middle of it all.

He lit the fire and made us two hot chocolates. We sat together on the couch as the flames crackled away.

"What's going on with your mother and you?" he asked. "I've always known she's overprotective but she seems to go into overdrive whenever I'm around."

"Don't worry," I said, taking a sip of hot chocolate. "Mum's just being mum."

"Well," he said and touched my hand gently. "If she's worried that I'd hurt you, I wouldn't. I've grown up a lot since we broke up."

"Well," I said, setting my hot chocolate back down. "We both have."

He gave me a lingering look and a troubled

expression came over his face. I wished I knew what he was thinking.

"Are you cold?" he asked and went out of the room.

He returned with a patchwork blanket and wrapped it over both of our laps. "What I meant to say is that there's never been a single day that I haven't regretted my actions. I know we agreed to be friends but I can't help wonder what it would have been like if we hadn't broken up..."

The words hung in the air as he leaned in closer and stretched out a hand to tuck a stray hair behind my ear. My breath caught in my throat. I wouldn't have stopped him if he had kissed me, but where would that lead to? Was I ready for this? Could we just forgive the past and move on? A little voice at the back of my mind, Mum's voice, told me it was better to let old ghosts rest.

I took my hand in his. "But we can't, can we?"

"I know but I can't help wondering…" he paused and looked away. "If only I'd sent that letter to you."

"Do you still have it?" I asked, curiosity getting the better of me.

He fetched a shoebox from upstairs and we looked through it together. It was full of old photographs of us, shells that we collected, a woven bracelet I had made him and the letter.

"I can't believe that you kept these old things,"

I said.

"Of course," he said, putting his arm around me. "These things meant a lot to me - they still do." It felt natural for him to hold me like this - like we were an old couple who'd been together forever. The opposite of how I remembered things with Nick. I shrugged away the thought as he put the letter into my hand.

"I'll read it later," I said, placing it on the coffee table.

We chatted the hours away and I could have easily fallen fast asleep on his shoulder.

Michael smiled at me as I yawned. "Will you let me take you home?" he asked.

"Yes, okay," I said, trying to shake off my

tiredness.

"Don't forget the letter," he said, handing it to me.

Neither of us spoke on the drive home until he pulled up outside the café.

"You know where I am," he said. He leaned in as if he was going to kiss me, then fixed his eyes behind me.

I followed his gaze and saw Mother, standing at the doorway, dressing gown and slippers on, with her arms folded across her chest.

"Well, I'd better go," I said, hurrying out of the car and waving him goodbye.

"Mum," I said, walking away from her and into the flat. "I really don't want to have an argument with you. I'm tired."

Mum followed me upstairs into the kitchen with a look like she was demanding an explanation.

"Tea?" I sighed and she shook her head.

I filled up the kettle with my back turned to her. "Aurora," she said. "I just hope that you know what you're getting yourself into."

I switched the kettle on and got a cup out of the cupboard. "Look whatever is or is not happening between Michael is none of your business."

"And what about Nick? Don't you think that you're being selfish? A baby needs its father, Aurora. You've got responsibilities."

I sighed as the kettle boiled and I poured the

water on my tea. "Look," I said. "Mother, I'm well aware of my responsibilities. The fact is that despite everything, I've had an enjoyable evening and I don't want to spoil it with an argument. I'm going to bed." I took my tea and curled up on my bed with the letter.

I opened it, smiling at my name written in Michael's looped handwriting. My heart jumped when I read it, it was far from the apology I had expected:

I'm glad that you're going away Aurora, I hope that you never come back. I stopped reading and shoved the letter back into the envelope. Tears welled up in my eyes. How could he write that to me and behave the way he had tonight? Why would he want me to read it in the first place when the words sounded so hateful? It made no sense. I would have to talk to him about it, but not tonight. Tonight, I wanted nothing more than to fall into a deep sleep and forget it all.

Chapter Eleven

The following morning my contractions began. I fished for my mobile to ring my midwife. She said it was too early to go to the hospital so I rested in bed, not wanting Mum to fuss about me. My phone rang and it was Rachel.

"Just wanted to see how your night went? I saw your mum coming over to sit beside you. I can't believe that she did that."

"Me neither," I said. "I went back to Michael's after the performance finished and we had a long talk. It was like it used to be. But then-" I paused thinking of the letter and his eagerness for me to read it.

"But?" she asked.

"Nothing, just stuff from the past," I said, not wanting to explain the letter to her. Another contraction came on. "Listen, I'm going to have to go. I'm in labour."

"Ooh, do you need anything? Want me to come over?"

"No," I said, grateful for her offer but not sure what she could do.

"Well, I'll let you go. Keep me updated and call me if you need anything."

"Will do," I said. No sooner had I said goodbye to her than Mum was knocking on the door.

"Aurora," she called. "Are you getting up today? There's a visitor to see you."

"Yes, I'll be there in a second," I grumbled and heaved myself out of bed, wrapping my dressing gown tightly around me.

I went to the living room, expecting to find Michael, but instead, standing in the middle of the room was Nick. Six foot tall, clipped black hair and designer-clad in a polo shirt and jeans, with that suave smile and baby blue eyes that would have once knocked me for six.

"What on earth are you doing here?" I asked.

"I had to see you," he said, coming closer for a hug. I backed away uncertainly and looked behind me to see Mum, standing in the doorway with a sheepish grin.

"I will just leave you two alone for a moment,"

Mum said, nodding and winking at Nick.

I shot her a dagger look. "No, stay Mother. Did you ask Nick here?"

"Well," she spluttered. "I... I only did what I thought was best."

Another contraction came, and I clutched my stomach. "You always think that you know best, but you don't Mum."

"Oh, you're in labour darling," she said, rushing towards me. "Everything will be alright, let me help you." She clutched my arm and ushered me to the sofa. I sat down and she crouched down on one side, Nick on the other side of me. His eyes fixed on my stomach with sheer panic spread across his face. "Are you having the baby? Now?"

"YES," I shouted back at him.

"Just take deep breaths my darling," Mum said.

"Just back off," I said, shrugging her off. "I can't believe that you would go behind my back like that."

"I'm sorry," she said, with tears in her eyes. "I just thought-"

"You'd just thought that you'd wade in as you always do," I sighed. "Well, I've had enough. As soon as I've recovered from the birth, the baby and I will move out." Never mind the house prices, I couldn't live in the same house as her now.

"Please Aurora-," Mum cried. "You don't mean that. I'm sorry I upset you. I just want you to try and make it up with Nick, for the baby's sake."

"Oh, you do, do you? I'm not sure that you would if you knew just what Nick has been up to."

Nick's face twisted in panic. "Aurora, darling, this is hardly the time or the place."

I shook my head and turned to Mum. "Do you think Amanda is his first affair? You must have read about Penny Jacobs, his co-star on *The Last Clan*. Traded me in for a younger model according to the press. That's how I found out about it. A bunch of pap's showing up on my doorstep."

Mum looked aghast. "I saw that in the paper, but you weren't speaking to me. Anyway, I thought you'd got over that, darling. Yes - he went off with Penny what's her name and this Amanda person but he's here now, doesn't that tell you something?"

"Yes, it tells me that Amanda has dumped him and he's come back to me with his tail between his legs."

Nick glanced at me like I had caught him out. "You're not thinking straight," he said. "Those were stupid, stupid mistakes. I was a long way away from you and Penny was just there."

"I suppose that Amanda was just there as well." I cried out with another contraction and squeezed his hand, making the skin turn white.

"Not so hard," he said. "I just had a manicure. Anyway, you know Amanda could never fill your shoes, Aurora."

"You mean she dumped you and you don't want to be alone."

"Well," he said, sweat glistening off his brow. "I wouldn't quite put it like that."

Mum eyed him with a shocked expression.

"You haven't heard the best bit yet Mum," I said. "There wasn't just Penny and Amanda. Tell her Nick, tell her about your affair with the make-up artist and then the model before Amanda. You paid to keep those affairs out of the press."

Nick's eyes burrowed into the carpet. "I can't

help it. I'll admit I've had some issues and I'm sorry. But I've worked through them now. I won't cheat on you again, Aurora. I'm a one-woman man from now on. I love you."

"You say that every time you come back, Nick," I said. "It doesn't mean anything anymore."

Mum narrowed her eyes at Nick and turned to me. "I'm sorry I should have listened to you when you said I should stay out of your business."

"Look, maybe I should go," he said.

"You're not going anywhere - owww!" I said, squeezing his hand tighter as wet patches appeared on the sofa. "My waters just broke.

The baby is coming!"

"The baby is coming!" he repeated stupidly, jumping away from me with a disgusted look on his face.

"Mum, will you get my overnight bag?" I asked, ignoring him.

She nodded and left the room.

Nick sat looking like a spare part. "What shall I do?"

"Nothing, please, just hold my hand."

I gripped his fingers tightly while the contraction went through me. The worst one yet. "This is all your fault, Nick."

"Well, it takes two," Nick quipped. A smug

smile appeared across his face. "I've just had a really brilliant idea. Why don't I drive you in your car to the hospital Aurora?" He looked at me as if he was waiting for me to applaud him.

"You can't drive!" I cried, looking at him like he was talking out of his hat.

Nick ran his fingers through his black hair. "I'll have you know that I have driven in many films."

"Yes, on the back of a lorry, this is real life," I said. *How on earth did I end up getting pregnant to this idiot?*

"Well," he said childishly. "It's practically the same thing."

I shook my head at him as Mum came back

with my overnight bag.

"Mum," I cried, "I need to go to the hospital. Call Colin now."

"I've tried, he's on a mountain hike, there mustn't be any signal and I don't know what time he'll be back."

"Ring an ambulance, then."

"I could, but it'll take over an hour to get here."

"Can we try Michael?"

Nick narrowed his eyes at me. "Who the bloody hell is Michael?"

"Michael's a friend," I said, giving him a dirty look. He had no right to ask me about the men in my life.

"Fine," Mum said and then she dialed the number. I heard her asking him to come over sharpish.

I thought I could hear Christmas music coming from outside just before Michael knocked.

Mum went to let him in. He stood in the living room, glancing at me with worry and totally ignoring Nick.

"Playing Santa?" I asked Michael, gawping at his Santa suit.

"Something like that," he said, taking his hand in mine. "Your chariot awaits my lady, although it might not be exactly what you had in mind."

"I don't care if we have to fly there in a hot-air balloon, as long as we get there," I said, and imagined with all the Christmas music that there was a sleigh outside.

Nick stood up next to Michael and puffed his chest out. "So, this is him," he said.

"Nick, Michael. Michael, Nick," I said looking from one to the other. Neither one of them offered the other a friendly greeting and they eyed each other with suspicion.

"I'm coming with you Aurora," Nick stated.

Michael gently took my hand to help me up. "Who do you want to go with you?" he asked. "I'm afraid that I can only take two people."

"Mum?" I replied. "Will you come with me?"

"Yes," she beamed. "Of course, my darling." She turned to Michael. "Your transport better not be a sleigh."

Michael chuckled and I looked away, imagining her face if there was a sleigh outside.

"What about me?" Nick asked with a sour expression.

"Here," said Mum, throwing him the keys. "You stay here and wait for Colin to come back."

We walked with Michael outside to find a sleigh just as I had pictured. Only instead of reindeer, two horses were pulling it. Magical I thought, glancing at the fairy lights and presents in the back. Curtains were already twitching across the street but I didn't care if all the town came out, as long as I got to the hospital.

Chapter Twelve

I glanced at Michael and back again. "I know I said I wanted you to get into the Christmas spirit, but don't you think that bringing a sleigh is a little extreme?"

Michael laughed. "I'm delivering the books to the competition winners. Your idea really boosted sales. I thought I'd deliver in style."

"That's great," I said, glancing at the people now gathering on the street. "But can you help me up into the sleigh before I give birth here with everyone watching?"

He helped me on to the sleigh, but Mum remained behind.

"You can't expect us to travel in that thing," she exclaimed. "Are those horses properly trained?"

The horses grunted and stamped their hooves.

"Come on, Mum," I cried. "There's no time to waste!"

"Fine," she said, hoisting herself up and ignoring Michael's offer of help. She narrowed her eyes at him. "But I hope you know how to drive this thing."

"Of course," said Michael, climbing into the front and tugging on the reins. "Off we go!"

We went through the streets with the Christmas music blaring and all the locals coming out of their houses to gawp.

In between all that and Mum telling me to keep breathing, my head was spinning.

We had just turned off into a country lane when I cried, "I need to push."

"Hang on," Mum called.

"We're nearly there," agreed Michael. "Can't you hold it in for a minute?"

"I can't," I cried. "I need to push. Now!"

Michael pulled over to the side of the road and dialed an ambulance.

"Right," he said with the phone still clamped to his ear. "The ambulance is on its way."

He came round to help with a smile that

couldn't hide the fear in his eyes as he held my hand.

"I don't think that the ambulance will get here in time," I cried.

"Don't worry," Mum said. "I'm always prepared for anything; you have to be in the café business."

"In the café business?" Michael asked, glancing at her in bewilderment.

"Yes," she said. "You wouldn't believe all the mess there is." She pulled a whole roll of kitchen towel and alcohol hand gel out of her bag.

"Right, give me the phone Michael," said Mum.

I lay across the sleigh seat with a blanket over

me. Mum took charge, cleaning her hands and talking to the person on the other end of the phone. She laid kitchen towel down underneath me and checked how far dilated I was.

"You're fully dilated," Mum cried, frowning with worry.

"I know," I screamed in agony, never having felt pain like it before. Michael murmured calmly that it was going to be okay and kept a tight hold of my hand.

"I can see the head," Mum said, her face peering at me from underneath the blanket. "You just need to give one more big push."

"I can't," I said, glancing from her to Michael

and then back again.

"Yes, you can," Mum said.

"You're so brave, Aurora. I'm so proud of you," Michael said.

I gritted my teeth and pushed as hard as I could. All three of us started sobbing as I felt the baby come out and give a loud cry.

"Well, we know that she's got a good set of lungs on her," Mum said. "Definitely a Winter."

Michael offered his jacket to wrap her in.

"Thanks," Mum said as she wrapped her in it and then placed her into my arms. "Aurora, meet your daughter."

"She's perfect," I said, holding her tiny little

fingers with mine.

"Yes," Mum agreed, kissing me on the head and smiling down at the baby. "Just like her mum."

Michael glanced down at the little bundle in my arms. "Aurora," he said. "She's beautiful."

The horses turned their heads and above the Christmas music, I heard the wail of the ambulance.

"Finally," Mum cried.

The wailing came closer as did the blue flashing lights. The paramedics got out and took the baby and me with Mum in the back of the ambulance. They wrapped the baby up in a blanket.

"You will come and see us, won't you?" I asked Michael, giving him his jacket back.

"Of course," he promised. I watched him waving away in his Santa suit as the ambulance doors were closed.

Chapter Thirteen

Colin and Nick arrived just as the midwife had checked me and the baby over.

Colin kissed me on the head and turned to the baby in my arms. "Hello, little one I'm Colin."

"Her honorary grandpa," I said and he looked over the moon.

Nick stood tentatively at the end of the bed. "Would you like to hold her, Nick?" I asked.

"Yes," he said and held the baby awkwardly. He glanced at her with what I'm sure were tears in his eyes, when his phone started to ring.

"Sorry," he said, handing her back to me. "I've got to take this."

He shuffled out the room and I suspected it was a work call. Work always came first with him. I shouldn't have expected it not to at the birth of his daughter. We've got each other I thought as I cradled the baby in my arms. I can't explain the rush of love I felt for her. I realised she was going to need all of us. Me, her grandmother, her honorary grandpa Colin, even her father if he could make time for her.

"Let me have a hold of my grandchild?" Mum asked. She sang softly to the baby who fell fast asleep in her arms.

She placed her gently in her hospital cot and sat down beside Colin.

"What are you going to call her?" Colin asked and glanced out the window. I followed his gaze as a blizzard of snow started to fall. A robin sat on the window ledge looking right at me.

"What about Robin?" I suggested.

Mum tutted. "Robin? You can't call her that."

"Well, I think that it's a perfect name," Colin said.

Mum shot him a look like he should be quiet.

"Robin?" Nick asked, coming back into the room. "Did I hear you say you are going to call her Robin Hope?"

"Robin Winter Hope," I said, thinking I wanted to keep my mum's family name.

"That sounds perfect," Mum said.

"Do you think I could have a moment alone with Aurora?" Nick asked, glancing at me intently.

Mum glared at Nick.

"Can we just have a minute?" I asked Mum.

"Come on," Colin said to Mum. "Let's get a coffee."

Mum eyed Nick as if to say *I'm watching you*.

When they had gone Nick sat down on the edge of the bed. "That was my agent on the phone," he said. "I've got to go to London for an audition. Will I send my PA to help you pack everything up?"

"Pack everything up?" I asked, confused.

"Yes, for you and baby Robin, when you both come and live with me."

"I'm sorry, Nick," I said. "But I don't think I'm coming back to London. I might stick around Green Leaf for a while." Yes, Mum could be a bit of a pain sometimes, but I loved her and then there was Michael - the thought of being so far away from him again had my stomach in knots.

"Where does that leave us?" Nick asked.

"It doesn't, I guess. You'll always be Robin's father though. You can come back anytime you want to see her."

He smiled and looked a little relieved. "Right,"

he said. "Well, I'd better get going. The audition is first thing in the morning. They want to cast the part before Christmas. It's a big part, a lead role in a new rom-com. I'll try to come up and see Robin in the New Year. I'll call you."

I won't hold my breath.

Robin was still sleeping peacefully when Mum came back by herself. "I saw Nick, on the way out," she said. "So, he's headed back to London? Does that mean that things are definitely over between the two of you?"

"Yes, but he's still going to come back and see Robin."

"I think it's for the best," she said, and I stared at her in disbelief. Well, I suppose that there's a first time for everything.

"Where's Colin?" I asked.

"He's just having forty winks in the café. I think he's tired from all the mountain climbing," she said. A serious expression came over her face. "Aurora, I know it's your life. I'm sorry about trying to get you back together with Nick. I just thought it was the right thing to do. I didn't want you to be alone like I was when I had you. Your grandmother was there, of course, but I always felt her constant disapproval for having you young and not being married."

"Aww, Mum. I didn't know that."

"Yes, well, that's what your grandmother was like. I want to tell you the truth. I should have done it long since. Your father wasn't in the picture. He was a tourist passing through town. I only knew him for one week and by the time I realised I was pregnant he was long gone. I didn't have a phone number or address for him. Your grandma insisted on the lie that he was at sea. I suppose she was ashamed of me. When you asked about him, I didn't know what else to say. The truth is I have no idea where your dad is, or even if he's still alive. Do you think you can ever forgive me?"

I took her hands in mine. All the anger and pain I had built up about the absence of my father had subsided. I realised that as hard as it was for me to grow up without a father, it must have been twice as hard for her to bring me up alone, feeling my grandmother's disapproval.

"I'm not angry with you, I wish you'd told me the truth sooner. And I'm just sorry that you had to go through all that."

"I'm not," she said, the tears in her eyes matching my own. "I'd go through it a thousand times over if it meant that I could have you for a daughter. Colin's talked to me. I know I haven't been the easiest mother in the world lately. I'll try and change and stay out of your life. You won't move out, will you Aurora? You'll let me look after you, won't you?"

"Of course," I said. "We're family, aren't we? By the way, Colin is rather a nice man."

"Thank you, my darling," she said, kissing me on the cheek. "Your Michael looked quite sexy in a Santa suit, didn't he?"

"Mum, please," I laughed. "He's not *my Michael*. Anyway, I can't think about him like that right now. I've just given birth."

"Well, don't wait until you're old and grey like me to find the love of your life. Seeing the way he was with you when you gave birth made me realise how much he cares for you."

"I know," I said. "I care for him too." I thought of the letter he had written to me again and my stomach tightened. In all the chaos, I hadn't been able to ask him about it. I would, but for now, I just wanted to be with Robin and Mum. Right now, nothing else mattered.

Chapter Fourteen

"Someone's got an admirer," a nurse said carrying a balloon and a giant smiling teddy bear towards my bed.

"Thanks," I said, assuming they were from Nick.

The nurse placed the presents on my bed next to the chocolates and the baby shawl aunty Rachel as she called herself had brought in. I'd texted her as soon as I'd had a minute and she had come rushing up to the hospital. I was glad for her friendship. She knew what it was like to have just had a baby and reassured me I was doing things right.

After the nurse went to see another patient, I read the card that had come with the teddy bear: *You both looked so peaceful, I didn't want to wake you. Will come and see you as soon as you get home, love Michael xx*

My stomach flipped with disappointment and tears spilled from my eyes. I wiped them away and read the card again. My eyes resting on the words: *love Michael.* Did he love me? I thought he did, but maybe I was wrong. Anyway, he still had some explaining to do about the letter.

I tried to shrug off my doubts and texted him to thank him for the presents. I told him about the baby's name and put: *I hope that you will come and see us again. I'll let you know when I'm out of hospital xx*

I sent the text and glanced up to see Mum carrying a newspaper. "Look," she said, "You've made the front page of the *Green Leaf Gazette.*"

"Let me see that," I said, taking the paper and reading the headline: **A Special Sleigh Delivery** and a picture of Mum, Michael and me in the sleigh. Although I looked rather pained. Not my best look.

The whole of Green Leaf turned out to see Aurora Hope I read. *Estranged wife of actor Nick on her way to give birth…* thought he would get a mention.

"The café is even mentioned underneath,"

Mum said, interrupting my thoughts. "It'll be great publicity." Robin stirred from her sleep. Mum picked her up and kissed her on the forehead. "We should frame it for you, Robin, for when you're older." She paused and looked at the teddy bear and the balloon.

"Well," she said, reading the card. "That was nice of Michael, it's a shame that you two didn't manage to talk."

"I wish we had," I agreed, tears coming into my eyes. Mum put Robin back in her cot and sat on the edge of the bed with her arms around me. "Don't you worry about it. Things will work out. You'll see."

Chapter Fifteen

On Christmas morning, the doctor came round to tell me I could go home. Colin came to collect me and Robin. Mum had stayed at home to get everything ready. When I arrived back, I was under strict instructions from Mum to take it easy while she busied around in the kitchen.

Colin and I sat watching TV, fussing over baby Robin in her Moses basket with the smell of turkey wafting through the door.

"Is Michael coming over today?" Colin asked.

"I don't think so," I shrugged. "I texted him to wish him a Merry Christmas but I still haven't heard back from him." I hadn't heard back from the text I'd sent him in hospital either.

"Well, I'm sure that he will get in touch soon," Colin said. He glanced at Robin fast asleep in her Moses basket beside me on the sofa. "We'll have a lovely Christmas, just the four of us."

"Yes," I said. "We will."

Mum came in wearing a Christmas apron and with huge sparkly baubles hanging from her ears. "Are you going to help me in the kitchen, or not?" she asked Colin.

Colin got up slowly from the sofa.

"Well, chop-chop Colin," Mum said. "Those potatoes won't boil by themselves."

"No rest for the wicked," Colin laughed, and followed Mum into the kitchen. Five minutes later I heard Mum bossing him around. "Use the special Christmas plates Colin, not those old ones."

The doorbell rang, and Robin stirred from her sleep. I cradled her in my arms, about to get the door when Mum called, "Coming."

She appeared with Michael at the doorway. I ran a hand through my hair self-consciously, wishing I'd had the energy to do something other than tying it back in a scrunchie.

What a mess I must have looked in my nightie and dressing gown. In contrast to me, he had opted for a crisp clean white shirt and black woolly scarf. "I don't mean to intrude on your

Christmas," he said, with a smile that made his eyes sparkle. "I just wanted to drop these presents off for you and the baby."

I looked at the two Christmas gift bags. One had a robin on it, the other a polar bear with skates. "You shouldn't have," I said. "You already brought us gifts in the hospital."

"Nonsense," he said, handing me the gift bags. "The one with the polar bear on is for you."

"Thank you," I said, putting Robin back in her Moses basket.

"Now you're here. Why don't you stay for some dinner?" Mum suggested.

"I'll just get myself a sandwich at home," he

protested. "My sister couldn't come down from *Scotland* so I didn't see the point in making dinner for one."

"We can't have that," Mum said. "You'll stay. Now sit yourself down and I'll get you a coffee."

Michael did as he was told and Mum went back into the kitchen. I looked down at the presents.

"I hope that you haven't got us anything expensive. I haven't got you anything." Robin had so many things already. My eyes rested on the pile of gifts from Mum and her aunty Rachel, who had bought her a hamper full of baby shampoo, clothes, nappies and a big teddy bear. All the café regulars had brought her something and the knitting group had been busy making her little socks and booties.

I opened the presents to find that Michael had got the baby a snow globe with a robin inside and a beautiful sleepsuit with *Let it Snow* written on it. He had given me an adorable necklace with a robin on it.

I tried to put it on, but I was all fingers and thumbs. "Here, let me help you with that," he said.

He helped me on with the necklace, his fingers brushing against my skin making my heart thump in my chest.

Colin came in and put the coffees down. A scream came from the other room. "Colin, the turkey's stuck in the oven."

"Do you need any help?" Michael asked.

Colin shook his head. "Not to worry, I'll sort it out," he said, patting Michael on the shoulder.

Michael took his hands in mine. "I'm sorry I didn't reply to your texts. I thought I'd give you some space."

"That's okay, I'm glad that you're here now." I paused, thinking about the letter again. I had to ask him about it. It was now or never. "I read the letter you gave me. Why did you say you hoped I would never come back?"

He sighed. "Did you read the whole of the letter?"

"No," I admitted.

"It wasn't what you think. Can I read it to you

now?"

"Yes, it's in my room in my handbag at the bottom of my bed. Third door on the-"

"Right. I remember."

Both of us laughed.

Michael retrieved the letter and then sat back down and started reading it aloud. My heart was pounding.

He read: *I'm glad that you're going away Aurora, I hope you never come back. I say these words not because I don't love you. I do, the pain of losing you over the last few weeks has made me realise just how much. I wish I'd never thrown what we had away. I know we can't go back and we have to look to the future. So, go, expand your horizons, Aurora. I want you to live your dreams. I just hope that you carry me with you in your heart. Love always Michael xxx*

Tears trickled down my cheeks, and he wiped them away with his fingers. "I want us to be together Aurora. Having you back here has made me realise I still love you. I think you love me as well." He glanced towards the baby. "And I love baby Robin already."

"Yes, I love you," I said. "But I want to take things slow."

"Of course," he said, leaning in and giving me a kiss.

Our lips parted and we both looked at Robin

with love in our eyes.

"Come on you lot, Christmas dinner is on the table," Mum called from the kitchen. "I hope you're hungry."

He took my hand and with the other, carried baby Robin through in her basket. We sat at the table surrounded by turkey and all the trimmings. Robin murmured softly and I smiled at her. This really was my best ever Christmas.

The End

A Proposal for The Leaves of Change Café

Book Two in the Leaves of Change Café Series

By Sarah L Campbell

Chapter One

In the flat above *The Leaves of Change Café*, I held Robin, my seven-week-old baby daughter, in my arms. "Your father has missed out on so much," I said. She smiled up at me, blissfully unaware of the letter from her father's solicitor that lay on the table behind us.

It said, solicitor jargon aside, that her father, my soon-to-be ex-husband, Nick, wanted nothing to do with her, relinquishing access or words to that effect. Of course, there would be a handsome financial settlement as well as child maintenance. I suppose he thought I should be grateful. I knew all too well that nothing could make up for not having your father in your life. Nick hadn't seen her since she was born at Christmas. I had sent him emails about her. He hadn't replied to any of them. Now the letter confirmed my worst fears. He had abandoned her.

I swallowed down my tears as I heard Mum's familiar footsteps on the stairs. She popped her head around the door in her blue flowery patterned apron. "Why don't you come downstairs, love?" she asked, handing me a big red envelope.

"Thanks," I said, taking it from her to find it was a card with a baby bear and mummy bear cuddling up and having a cup of tea. It read: *Happy Valentine's Day Mummy, love Robin. xx.* "You shouldn't have bothered Mum."

"It was all Robin's idea. I just bought the card for her," Mum smiled.

I hugged her, putting the card next to the one that Mum had got from Colin with two intertwined swans on it.

Robin grizzled in my arms.

"Why don't you go downstairs and I'll look after her for a bit?" Mum asked. "You look like you could do with a break. I'm sure Patricia will get you whatever you fancy. I've made chilli con carne with rice for today's special..." Mum trailed off as her gaze rested on the letter on the coffee table. "What's this? More junk mail?"

"No, it's a letter from Nick's solicitor. You can read it-"

Before I had the chance to finish, she sat down beside me on the sofa, reading it and sighing at various intervals.

"Well, at least he's providing for her. That's the first decent thing that he's done."

"That's all I expected of him," I blurted out. "I mean, he's hardly going to be *father of the year*, is he?"

"No, but I thought…" She paused, as her eyes met mine and she smiled. "Ah, well, she doesn't need him. We'll manage just fine without him."

"Yes." I swallowed a lump in my throat. "I just want the divorce to be sorted so that we can all get on with our lives."

"Anyway," Mum said, folding the letter in half with a sharp crease and putting it back in the envelope on the coffee table. "Get your solicitor to write him a letter to tell him you agree. That should get things moving." She held her arms out towards Robin. "Shall I take her now?"

"Fine," I said, handing over my daughter. "I'll go downstairs and have something to eat. Will that please you?"

"I'm only thinking of you. Anyway, I've been wanting a cuddle from her all morning." As soon as I handed her to Mum, Robin fell quiet. Mum seemed to have a knack with her that I didn't. I went downstairs and through the side interconnecting door that led to the café.

Patricia stood behind the counter, taking the

tray of strawberry cheesecakes out of the display cabinet which was full to the brim with muffins, brownies, scones, Victoria sponge cake, and heart-shaped raspberry and vanilla cupcakes. The latter, an added addition for Valentine's Day.

She cut a thick wedge of strawberry cheesecake and placed it on a mismatched china plate before glancing up. "You look tired, not surprising. I remember just what it was like to have a new baby."

I looked up at the grey wisps of hair that had come loose from her sleek ponytail. She must be over sixty now, but I still saw a thirty-odd-year-old woman standing in front of me.

"Yes, does it ever get any easier?" I asked.

"Yes, but then you get toddler tantrums and the teenage years. My daughter Emily seemed to turn into a teenager from the age of ten," she laughed. "My son Eric, on the other hand never grew up. His wife rings me up from *America* to complain he's a slob."

"So much to look forward to," I smiled ironically.

"Don't you know it. Take a seat and I'll bring you something to eat. How about chilli con carne with rice and one of those heart-shaped raspberry and vanilla cupcakes seen as though it's Valentine's Day?"

"Go on then," I said.

Patricia went back behind the counter to sort

out my lunch. "Is Michael, taking you out somewhere nice for Valentine's Day?"

I frowned. "Yes, although I don't know where he won't tell me about it."

"A surprise, eh? Well, you don't look overly excited by it."

"I'm just worn out with Robin – I don't know if I have the energy to go out."

"Oh, I'm sure you'll enjoy it once you get there." She disappeared into the kitchen and I sat down at my favourite table by the window. Mum had added heart patterned tablecloths, in place of the usual flowery ones.

"Hope so," I replied as Miss Wilson came in, her terrier Bootles panting at her side.

"Hello, Miss Wilson," I said. Miss Wilson, a woman in her fifties, had a perfect blonde bob and an array of different tartan outfits. Today she had chosen a pleated skirt and jacket that matched Bootles's dog jacket. No one knew why she always wore tartan. *Maybe she's got Scottish ancestry or maybe she just really likes tartans*, I thought.

Patricia came back with the chilli con carne, the cake and a pot of tea with milk in a ceramic jug.

Miss Wilson eyed my food. "I think I'll have that as well."

"Great," Patricia said, making a note of it.

"Lovely. I'll just be here," Miss Wilson said,

pointing to a table next to mine. "Come on Bootles." She dragged the little terrier away, licking his lips.

I picked at my lunch, while Patricia brought Bootles a bowl of water and a dog biscuit. He sat on the chair beside his owner, as he always did. Miss Wilson leaned across the table towards me. "Where's that baby daughter of yours?"

"Upstairs with Mum," I said.

"I bet you're glad of the break. It isn't easy, is it? They just hand you your baby and expect you to know what to do like you have a manual." Her eyes clouded over with sadness, lost in her own thoughts.

I guessed she'd be thinking of her own daughter, Lucy. She died at 17 from leukemia. I remembered her being in hospital when I was in the sixth form. Miss Wilson never came to the café for two months after she died and when she did again, she never mentioned it.

A woman came through the door, dressed in shiny pink stilettos and a skintight cherry red dress. She strutted to the counter, teetering on her heels with a pile of papers in her hand. The conversations stopped dead around her. Instinct told me I knew this woman, although I couldn't place her. I dismissed the thought - probably one of Nick's friends who flattered his ego and in return, he'd charmed them into bed.

As I got up to serve her, Patricia came out of

the kitchen looking flustered.

"I'll serve her, don't worry," I said.

"Oh, you're an angel but I'd better do it," Patricia said. "Don't want your mum to complain that I'm making you work when you should be having a rest."

"Honestly, the way Mum goes on you'd think I was made of glass."

"Just enjoy it while it lasts," she said and turned back to serve the woman.

"Glad to finally get some service around here," the woman snapped at Patricia. "I'll have two lattes, a tuna salad and a chicken pie,"

I shook my head and returned to my seat.

Patricia hurried back to the kitchen while the woman impatiently drummed her fingernails on the counter.

Miss Wilson raised her eyebrows at me, and I gave her a look that said *tell me about it. Who was this woman?*

Patricia returned with her salad in a box, the chicken pie wrapped in a paper bag and made her drinks, handing everything over to her.

Bootles jumped down from his spot beside Miss Wilson and made a beeline for the woman at the counter just as she turned to leave. He danced around her as if she had a treat, causing her to stumble on her heels and drop the pile of papers that she had been juggling in one hand, with the food and drinks in the other.

"Down Bootles," Miss Wilson scolded.

Bootles bent his ears back and whined as Miss Wilson returned him to the chair. "Now, settle yourself down and be good," Miss Wilson said.

I wondered if I should help pick up the woman's papers, but her frosty expression told me I shouldn't.

"Let me help you with that," Miss Wilson said, returning to help her.

"Oh, there's no need. I can manage," the woman hissed, snatching up the papers and shoving them close to her chest. "Just control your animal next time."

Miss Wilson's face reddened as the woman huffed and marched out of the café, jangling the bell almost off its hinges.

"Well," Miss Wilson remarked. "Someone got out of bed on the wrong side this morning."

"Yes, rude. She's probably one of those miserable city types," Patricia called from the counter. "Sounded like a London accent."

"Probably came up here for a holiday," another customer, wiry-haired Alison Planter piped up. A prim woman in her early forties who ran the local florist shop.

"Yes, and by the sound of her, she needs it," Patricia added, and I smiled.

Miss Wilson asked Alison how she was

settling in her new home and I lost myself in my thoughts, still trying to place the woman who had marched out of the café moments earlier.

I mentally ran through a list of all Nick's conquests. I didn't recall her, but I knew her from somewhere.

I finished my lunch and headed back upstairs to find Robin fast asleep on the sofa in her Moses basket and Mum dozing off in the chair.

"Oh, Aurora, there you are," she said. "I wasn't asleep. I just closed my eyes for five minutes."

"Don't worry about it. You've got the magic touch," I said.

Mum shrugged indifferently. "It just comes

from years of practice." She got up from her chair. "Why don't I make us both a cup of tea and then we can have a little chat?"

By that, I presumed she'd be giving me a grilling about my evening with Michael later.

"Is he taking you somewhere nice?" Mum asked, returning five minutes later with the teas and plonking herself down beside me on the sofa.

"Michael?"

"No, a Hollywood movie star. I wish," Mum scoffed, curling her hands around her teacup.

"He's said it's somewhere special, that's all that he'll tell me."

"Oh, you're so lucky. I wish I was going off to a

fancy restaurant."

"You don't have to babysit. I mean I could cancel if you wanted to go out with Colin." It would give me the perfect excuse not to go. The last thing I felt like doing was getting all dolled up to go to a *fancy* restaurant. Anyway, I'd not been on a proper date with Michael since I'd given birth to Robin. Even as I thought about it, I could feel the nerves settling in.

"Nonsense, it's all arranged now," Mum said, casting a critical eye over me as if she was appraising a horse. "You'll have to wear something nice."

I frowned, presuming she was referring to my preference for wearing leggings and baggy tops. They were practical and comfortable.

"I mean anything that will actually *fit* you," Mum added. "You really should have let me take you shopping."

"Thanks, Mum," I said sarcastically. I could always rely on her to make me feel better about the added baby weight I hadn't lost yet. Subtlety was never her strong point.

"I'll have to see what I have in my wardrobe." I began thinking of the maternity clothes I had. Only one suitable dress and I had worn that at Christmas. Michael had already seen me in that.

"You can borrow something of mine if you'd like," Mum said, gulping down her tea.

"Thanks," I said politely. Me and her had very

different tastes. Her wardrobe was full of flowery t-shirts, dresses, or over the top glitzy things. I preferred simple clothes, basic patterns and one colour dresses.

She grimaced. "Alright don't look so horrified. I know you think that your mother has no taste."

"It's not – I don't think that," I said, trying to recover myself, realising that my inner thoughts had a habit of showing on my face.

"It's fine," she said. "I'm not offended." *She certainly looked it.*

Happily, my mobile phone beeped. A welcome distraction.

Mum smiled knowingly. "Oh, speak of the devil. I suppose that's Michael now, is it?"

Rachel texted: *Can you meet me tomorrow in Evergreen? I know it's short notice but I really need to talk? xx*

10 am okay? xx I replied.

"It's Rachel," I said. "She wants to meet tomorrow."

"Oh, right," Mum said. "Everything alright?"

"I think so," I said, guilt creeping up on me. Since Robin had been born, I had only seen Rachel, my old teenage best friend, briefly, if she came into the café or if I popped over for a quick coffee at her cottage. Usually, we'd end up talking about the kids. It felt like an eternity since we'd sat down and had a proper girly chat.

My mobile phone bleeped with another text: *Yes, look forward to it xx* Rachel replied.

"Right," Mum said, getting up from the chair with a small groan. "Well, I suppose that I'd better go back down. I've been a lot longer than I said I would, and Patricia will be desperate for her lunch by now. See you later."

Mum's footsteps back down the stairs stirred Robin from her nap.

"Come here my lovely," I said, picking her up and taking her through to my bedroom, which had the addition of a cot since there were only two bedrooms in the flat.

I fed Robin and put her in her baby bouncer and I rifled through my wardrobe. Every dress that I pulled out felt too dressy or too plain. Some of the dresses I had were a hangover from the starry occasions, like red carpet events I used to attend with my husband Nick. I didn't miss those days, wearing a forced smile for the camera while Nick lapped up all the attention, promoting his latest film role.

My hand rested on a strapless blue gown when the rude woman from the café came into my mind again. *Michelle, that was her name, Michael's ex-fiancée.*

I remembered I had seen her in a photograph in Michael's office at Christmas. What was she doing here in Green Leaf? For a holiday? To see Michael? He hadn't mentioned that she was coming to visit. Maybe she had just turned up out of the blue. I thought back to her order; she had ordered for two, two lunches, two coffees… for her and Michael? I told myself to stop running away with my thoughts. Michael would surely explain everything tonight.

Chapter Two

"Have you still not found anything to wear?" Mum asked, barging into my room. She still hadn't learned to knock.

"No, I haven't had time," I replied, picking up Robin from her changing mat and holding her to me.

"Goodness me," she tutted. "You've had all afternoon. Nothing fits you, I'm right, aren't I?"

"No," I lied. "Just nothing that I fancy."

Up went her eyebrows. "Come with me, we'll sort something out for you." She turned and left the room.

I followed her into her bedroom, sitting on the edge of her bed, while she rifled through her huge double cream wardrobe with bronze handles.

"Right," she said, pulling out a sleeveless pink dress with a tropical patterned print that made me wince.

"There's no need to say anything," she said. "I can tell by your face that you don't like it."

"It's not really my style." Better I thought than saying, *I'd not be seen dead in it.*

Next, she pulled out a long blue flowery, floaty skirt and a red wine satin dress that looked as if it had time travelled from the 90s. I didn't like it either.

"What's going on here?" Colin appeared in the doorway, dressed from head to toe in leathers.

Mum looked him up and down with a critical gaze. "Operation Aurora's night out, that's what. Been out on your bike again, I see?"

"Yes, and before you start - I only went up and down the coast with a few of my friends."

"Right, well I'm not going to have a go." *Unusual for her.* She hated him riding on that thing. "If you want to go riding around on that death trap, then that's your business. I'm much too busy trying to sort this one," she continued, her gaze falling back on me. "Oh, and Colin, while you're on your feet, there's a drip that needs fixing under the kitchen sink."

"I shall just get changed first if that's alright your ladyship," he grinned.

Mum laughed drily. Colin came closer, pulling Mum in for a big kiss.

She pulled away, rolling her eyes. "Oh, don't try my patience. Colin, go and get changed, will you? I've got things to do here."

"As you wish." He gave a mock bow and winked at me before leaving.

I stifled a laugh.

"Honestly, that man," she muttered with a thin smile. "Seen as though I didn't get a present this morning, I bet he got me a cheap bottle of plonk and flowers from the garage on the way home. That'll be my Valentine's Day gift."

I saw him wrapping up something in a suede box that looked like jewellery this morning, but I didn't want to tell her and spoil the surprise.

"Anyway, let's get back to the task in hand." She turned back to the wardrobe. "Ah-ha," she said, clapping her hands. "This is the one." She got out of the wardrobe a plain sleeveless knee-length strappy black dress with beading around the neckline. Her brow furrowed as she held the dress up against me. "Yes, this will fit you. You'll not remember Aurora, but I used to wear that dress to go clubbing in."

I remembered her dropping me off at Rachel's mum's house for a sleepover in that dress before her evenings out. I'd forgotten just how much I loved those nights. Rachel and I staying up late, sharing sweets and watching rented videos.

"Aurora," she said, bringing me out of my thoughts and shoving the dress in my hand. "Try it on and see what it looks like, preferably before Michael gets here. I'll take Robin now, shall I?"

"Fine," I said, handing her over.

"We're going to have a lovely evening, aren't we, Robin?" Mum asked my baby, kissing her on the head.

I took the dress back to my room and held it against myself in the mirror. Perhaps it wasn't modern, but vintage was all the rage, and this almost was. I rifled in my wardrobe and chose a strappy black pair of shoes and a clutch bag to match.

My heart sank when I returned from the shower and found I could not get the zip of the dress over the back of my nursing bra.

"Come on," I shouted in frustration when I heard a buzz on my mobile phone. That would be Michael. He'd probably knocked, but I couldn't hear a thing over Colin cursing to himself and banging about in the kitchen. Clearly, the drip under the sink proved to be a problem.

Mum knocked on my bedroom door. "Someone's knocking at the flat door and is that your mobile phone I can hear?"

"I'm coming," I shouted.

"I'll get it shall I?" she asked, her tone acidic.

"Alright," I shouted back, breathless. "I'm nearly there." Since when did putting on a dress begin to feel like an Olympic activity?

Five minutes later, Mum barged into my room. "Michael's here, he's watching Robin for a minute-" she began and paused, looking at me with concern.

"Mum, I can't..." I trailed off, too flustered to speak and pointed to the back of the dress.

"Oh, darling. Let me help." I stood up, and she stood behind me, giving the dress a sharp tug. I heard what I hoped was the zip going up and not the fabric ripping.

"There, it just needed a firm hand."

I smiled in relief as she handed me a tissue. "Now, fix your make-up. I'll keep Michael company until you're ready. Colin is in the kitchen. Despite all the noise he's been making, there's still a drip. I'll just have to fix it myself. Right, are you okay now? See you in a minute?"

"Yes," I nodded.

She left, and I dabbed a spot of powder over my reddened cheeks, wondering why I'd bothered to apply blusher in the first place. I grabbed the concealer, which claimed to remove dark circles from under the eyes, but mine still came through visibly after using it. Clearly not the magic worker it claimed to be. I added pink lipstick, painting on a smile and going into the living room.

"There she is," Mum said, eyeing me as I came into the room. As she got up to hug me, she whispered. "You look beautiful, even better than me in that dress."

"Thanks." For once she had said the right thing and gave me the confidence boost that I needed.

"Yes, you look beautiful," Michael said, holding Robin. I smiled, thinking what a natural he was with her. Mum took Robin while he fumbled in a carrier bag, pulling out an enormous bunch of red roses that must have cost him a fortune.

"Thanks, Michael," I said, trying to smile as he

handed them to me. Any other woman might have loved them, but they stirred up unpleasant memories for me of Nick. Every time he cancelled on me because of work or more usually rushing off to see another woman, an enormous bunch of roses would arrive at the house. I grew to hate those flowers and what they meant.

"Oh, aren't they just lovely," Mum exclaimed, glancing at them in admiration.

"Yes,", I said, trying to dismiss the memory. "I'll put them in water."

I went into the kitchen, searching for a vase under the sink, eyeing a cloth on the pipe and a bucket underneath it, half-filled with water.

Pots and pans bubbled away in the background. Something with the distinct smell of garlic.

I reached for an ancient, cut-glass crystal vase and turned back to the cooker.

"French onion soup," Colin explained, catching my curious gaze. "The first course before my pièce de résistance, steak and potatoes." His gaze rested on the flowers. "From Michael, I take it? What a lovely thought. I still haven't given your mum her present yet."

"I'm sure Mum will appreciate it and all the trouble you've gone to."

"Let's hope so. It might take her mind off my disastrous DIY."

I filled the vase with water, arranged the flowers in it and set it down in the centre of the kitchen table with a sniff, still thinking how much I hated red roses.

Colin caught my eye. "What is it, love? Are you worried about going out tonight?"

"A little," I said, not wanting to get into all that business about the flowers.

"Don't you worry, Robin will be fine with her grandma and her honorary grandpa."

"No doubt. Anyway, to her you're her real grandpa," I said, as the soup started boiling over.

Colin smiled and sorted out the soup. I returned to the living room, where Michael and

Mum looked to be in deep conversation. Robin lay in Michael's arms with a soft toy giraffe beside them.

"I was just quizzing Michael about where you might be going tonight," Mum said. "But he's remaining tight-lipped."

I shook my head, eyeing the giraffe. "You've got to stop buying her presents, Michael." Only this week he had bought her a night light that played music and projected stars onto the ceiling.

"Well, I couldn't very well get her mum something and not her, could I?"

"It's a lovely thought. You spoil her," I laughed.

"Hardly," he grinned and Mum took Robin from

him before he stood up, taking his hand in mine. "Are you ready to go?"

"Yes," I said, giving Robin one last hug.

Michael patted Robin on the head. "Bye-bye, little one."

Robin took no notice, far too engrossed in Mum waving the giraffe in front of her.

"Mum," I said, kissing her on the cheek. "I've left you a schedule on the fridge of when Robin needs to go to sleep and when she needs to be fed."

"Babies don't need schedules," Mum said crossly. "They just need love."

I shook my head at her.

"What? I raised you alright without schedules, didn't I?"

"Dinner's nearly ready," Colin called from the doorway, eyeing me and Michael. "You two not off yet?"

"Just going," I said, crouching down beside the sofa, telling Robin to be good. I glanced back to Mum nervously. "You will call if there's anything that comes up, won't you?"

"Oh of course," Mum said. "But I'm sure that there won't be. Now go on." She shooed me away with her hands. I kissed Robin again, guilt rearing its ugly head at leaving my baby for the first time. I took a deep breath and reminded myself she'd be fine with Mum and Colin.

Michael waved Robin goodbye. When we reached the flat doorway, he carefully placed the black silk wrap I had chosen to go with my dress around my shoulders.

"Such a gentleman," I said.

"Of course," he smiled.

I glanced back up the stairs, wondering if I shouldn't just cancel the whole evening.

Michael caught my eye as if he had guessed my thoughts. "You know that we don't have to go out if you don't want to, don't you?"

"I want to go," I said. "It's just, it's hard-"

"To leave Robin. for the first time," he finished. "Of course, it must be. She couldn't be in safer hands, though."

I took a deep breath. "No, you're right," I said. "Let's go and have a nice meal."

We got into the car and he drove out of the little high street, passing the row of shops, with all the shutters down for the night and took the turnoff for the coast road.

"Now I am intrigued," I said, wondering if he was taking the back road to Evergreen. "Aren't you going to tell me where we're going?"

Michael's smile widened. "Well, if I told you, then it wouldn't be a surprise, would it?"

"No, I guess not."

Read the rest in A Proposal for the Leaves of Change Café out now in eBook, coming soon to Paperback. Also coming soon, A Double Wedding for the Leaves of Change Café …

If you would like to catch up with me before the next book is published you can do so by following me on:

Facebook:

https://www.facebook.com/SarahLCampbel lAuthor/

Twitter:

https://twitter.com/SarahLCamWriter/

Instagram:

https://www.instagram.com/sarahlcamwrit er/

Lots of cat photos and updates about my work are on my social media.

You can also find me on my website: https://www.sarahlcampbell.com/

and sign up for my new newsletter here.

Other Titles by Sarah L Campbell

<u>*For Teenagers*</u>

Claire's Diary

<u>*For 9-12 year old's*</u>

Forty Cats

<u>*For 7-9 years old's The Fairy Imelda Series (eBook)*</u>

Fairy Imelda and a Wish for William (Book 1)

Smoky's Flying Adventure (Book 2)

Fairy Flutterberry's Worst Christmas (Book 3)

UK Readers:

NB: Claire's Diary and Forty Cats are available at Amazon UK and International and also at a range of online stores. The

Fairy Imelda series is available on Amazon Kindle.

Printed in Great Britain
by Amazon

31939134R00138